THE *Inheritance*

MARIE MALONE

ISBN 979-8-88685-967-6 (paperback)
ISBN 979-8-88685-968-3 (digital)

Copyright © 2023 by Marie Malone

All rights reserved. No part of this publication may be reproduced, distributed, or transmitted in any form or by any means, including photocopying, recording, or other electronic or mechanical methods without the prior written permission of the publisher. For permission requests, solicit the publisher via the address below.

Christian Faith Publishing
832 Park Avenue
Meadville, PA 16335
www.christianfaithpublishing.com

Printed in the United States of America

1

As the sun set across the vast prairie, John Wilkes leaned on the old fence and admired the beautiful scenery. He often spent his evenings in this his favorite spot on the ranch. It was a time for reflection and quiet time with God and his prayers. A breeze swept through, cooling him off for a moment. He looked at all the buildings on his property—the tall red barn where hay was stored, the long stables where many of his horses were comfortably enclosed, the older sheds where his hay equipment and tractors were stored, the rambling two-story ranch home surrounded by tall imposing oak trees. He had so many memories of happier times in that old house. His wife, Margorie, could always be seen washing the dishes or peeling the potatoes for supper. She had sadly passed away four years ago of a sudden disease. His two sons, Jake and Justin, grew up in that house. Now it was only occupied by himself and his sweet daughter-in-law, Stephanie. John sincerely had hoped to pass this wonderful ranch down to his sons one day, and now it weighed heavily on his heart as to what would happen to it once he passed on.

Stephanie and Jake had married last summer under the tall oak trees in the backyard. It was a fabulous ceremony and celebration of love. Then a tragic accident six months ago claimed the life of his son Jake, leaving him and his daughter-in-law all alone in the house. Stephanie had decided to stay with him after Jake's death as she really grew to love the ranch and didn't have a desire to leave it. She put as much work into the running of the ranch as any hired hand would have done. Her garden was just starting to produce vegetables for the picking. She always said that she wanted to plant a garden, and having grown up in the city, this was her first chance to work the soil and grow something of her own. She often said working in the garden renewed her faith and helped her deal with the sorrow of losing her life's love.

The accident happened on a cold day in December. Jake had been rounding up some cattle, and suddenly something had spooked the horse he was riding, causing him to fall off, hitting his head on a stone and ending his life. It was so unexpected that it still was hard to deal with. Yet another reflection and a request for peace in his evening prayers. Stephanie and Jake had wanted a large family and were thinking of starting their family this summer, but now that dream had ended.

John stood up straight and headed for the welcoming lights of the house, wondering how he was going to go on. His family ranch had been Wilkes family ground for over one hundred years. He needed to know that it would stay in the family, but how was that going to happen now, with the inheritance at risk.

John opened the back door and smelled something delicious. His daughter-in-law was an excellent cook, so dinner promised to be delicious once again.

Shaking off the cool evening breeze, stomping his boots to remove the caked-on mud, and removing his hat, he looked around the kitchen for Stephanie.

"Hello? Stephanie?" *Where is she?* He walked over to the stove and removed the lid on a simmering pot. Aw, delicious-smelling warm stew—his favorite.

"Sorry, Dad," Stephanie called as she came in from the other room. "I was on the phone with Trina. We were just catching up on our day."

Trina was a neighbor just up the road. She was married to Brian, the son of his friend Tom. Trina and Brian had lived up the road about three years now. Married with a small son, Bobby, they were a nice set of neighbors to have. Trina and Stephanie had grown close when she and Jake married last summer. She had been a constant source of comfort for Stephanie after Jake died.

THE INHERITANCE

"Oh, that is good. How are they coming along with preparing for baling?"

"Well, fine, I guess. Trina and I tend to gossip more than we should sometimes, I think," Stephanie replied as she started to set the table for dinner. "How about you, Dad? Is there anything I can help with tomorrow?"

"No, I think everything is set. Since it is a Saturday, there are some strong able-bodied boys from the high school coming to help with the baling."

God always provided some young men willing to work to earn a little spending money by helping local farmers on the weekends. And since school finished for the summer, John was hoping to find one or two of those young men to employ over the summer. Tomorrow's hot, sticky, itchy day would determine which boys would be offered the chance to come work on the Wilkes's ranch.

They sat down for dinner. John said a prayer for the food and asked God's blessings on his family and for endurance to get the baling done tomorrow.

"Dad, can I ask you a question?" Stephanie inquired.

"Sure, dear, what is it?"

Stephanie seemed to have a hard time finding the words to say.

"I know that you have things under control here on the farm, and Trina mentioned that Mrs. Stevens was looking for some help at the library. She is apparently planning to have a knee replacement and would need someone to cover the library over the summer. How would you feel about me inquiring about the position?"

Stephanie had completed her four-year degree in education right before she and Jake got married. Jake had convinced Stephanie to wait to apply for a teaching position until they were settled on the farm.

"Well, that sounds like an interesting proposition and something that would be right up your alley," John replied. "I think you should check it out. It might help to see other people besides my old wrinkled face every day." He chuckled.

"Okay, I will then."

3

"This stew is delicious once again," John commented as he helped himself to a second helping.

After dinner, John went to watch the news on TV while Stephanie cleaned up the dinner dishes. The news was never encouraging anymore, it seemed, but one had to be prepared and knowledgeable on the happenings of the world.

As the news rolled on, a commercial came on about a new veterinary hospital and clinic. It appeared it was slated to be open in September. John listened intently, and then the big shock—a picture of one of the new vets. It was his son Justin, whom he hadn't seen or heard from in four years.

2

The memories came flooding back. It was the day of his sweet Margorie's funeral, and several neighbors and family were gathered in the family home reminiscing about Margorie. While it was a very sad day and he wished with all his might that she was there also, John soaked in all the condolences and voices of sympathy. How was he going to go on without her? His boys were away at college when their mother had been diagnosed with Lou Gehrig's. They didn't witness the day-to-day struggle that she had faced. Now she was at peace and no longer suffering. Jake was talking with a neighbor about the upcoming harvest season and finishing his last year at the university. Justin was rather quiet sitting alone in his mother's favorite rocker. Later, after all the visitors had left, John asked his sons to join him at the dining table. He had laid out his plans for the future, which included both of his sons taking over for him when they finished college. Jake had seemed accepting of that proposal, but Justin did not. He had finally spoken up, saying that he wished to pursue his interests off the farm by attending veterinary school. He wasn't interested in the running of the family ranch. The news had come as quite a shock to John. He had always assumed that his farm would continue in the family for many generations to come. Voices were becoming slightly elevated, and John had told Justin that he was expected to help his brother run the farm. It was the way it was going to go. Justin balked at the directive, and several hurtful remarks were exchanged between them, resulting in Justin leaving the house and returning to school. Jake had commented that he was just taking Mom's death hard and he would come around.

That harvest season was completed without Justin's help, and he had chosen not to come home for the holidays. Attempts to talk to his son were not received well. A bitterness arose between them. Finally, John had told Justin that when graduation occurred in the spring, that was the final tuition payment he was going to make. If Justin wished to pursue a veterinary degree, he would have to find the funding on his own. It was a harsh directive but one that John had felt would shake some sense into his son. They had not communicated since that time. John had known that Jake and Justin spoke intermittently; but Jake, other than telling his father all was going fine for Justin, hadn't shared any other news.

Now four years had passed. His son Jake was gone. His son Justin wasn't speaking to him. The family farm was getting to be too much for John to handle on his own with only occasional help. Justin had obviously finished his vet degree and seemed to be doing well with opening a new hospital and clinic. John resigned himself to the painful memories and lack of communication that he had contributed to as well.

The next morning Stephanie was excited as she left to go talk with Mrs. Stevens about the library position. John had not shared seeing the commercial with her. She had not met Justin but knew about the family discord between them. Justin had sent a gift to his brother and Stephanie but had chosen not to attend their wedding.

John prepared his mind and body for the arduous work of baling hay. His hired help would be arriving soon, and he needed to get the equipment ready to roll.

3

The day had been a scorcher. The sun had beat down on the balers, and even though several breaks had been given, everyone was ready for the long day to end. John thanked his hired help for the day and paid them generously for their help.

As he entered the kitchen, he could smell the delicious dinner being prepared. He really didn't know what he would have done if Stephanie had decided to return to her family. In agreeing to stay, he had not only an outstanding cook and housekeeper, he had a companion to share the quiet evenings with.

"How did your conversation with Mrs. Stevens go today?" John inquired.

"Very well," Stephanie replied. "She was receptive to the idea of me taking over for her but wanted to run the idea by the library board first. They meet next week, so she said she would let me know soon."

John knew that the position would give Stephanie some time to develop new friendships and was hoping she would be given the opportunity to work at the library.

After dinner and dishes, Stephanie and John were sitting in the living room nonchalantly watching the evening news when a commercial again appeared for the new vet hospital and clinic opening soon.

Stephanie lifted her head from the book she was pursing and looked over at John.

"Is that…Justin, your son's new facility?"

"Yes, it would appear so," John answered.

Stephanie continued to look inquiringly at John, so he tried to explain the circumstances to her.

"I'm sure Jake told you of our argument so many years ago that resulted in Justin not returning home?" At Stephanie's nod, John continued, "Justin had always enjoyed tending to the animals on the farm, but I guess I expected him to show more interest in the daily field work and not just animals. But he wanted nothing to do with baling hay or tilling the soil. He was often adamant that he had more interesting pursuits than sweating over the dry dirt, as he had put it, and would often deliberately find other things to keep himself occupied. I tried many times to encourage him, and it just never was his desire to work the farm. I tried to understand, but I guess it just kept eating away at me, and finally, I gave him an ultimatum. Well, it backfired, and now I have lost both of my sons." John finished tiredly, "I think I will go on to bed. It has been a very tiring day."

"Okay, Dad. I hope you sleep well," Stephanie replied.

As John left the room, an idea began to form in Stephanie's mind, and she decided to lift up a prayer to the good and gracious Lord.

* * * * *

Over the next few days, Stephanie worked on her plan in her mind, trying to figure all the pros and cons within it. She desperately wanted John to find peace and also some relief from the day-to-day that seemed to tire him more and more lately. She was definitely concerned about John's health and stamina in working the farm.

Her extended family had a farm in southern Iowa about four hundred miles away. Her brother, Seth, and cousins Mike and Steve worked together to make sure it was a profitable and lasting legacy. She knew that was what John had hoped for his place as well. After Jake died, Stephanie was lost and wasn't sure what she wanted to do. Should she have returned to her family's home in the city?

John had sat down with her and explained that she was a welcome and treasured part of the family place. He encouraged her to stay with him, and together they would persevere. He never pressured

THE INHERITANCE

her in any way but rather made her feel needed, and she had decided to stay on for the time being. The neighbors knew that Stephanie and John had leaned on each other and supported each other after the tragic passing of Jake. Now with the job opportunity at the library, she was beginning to lift herself out of the fog that seemed to have accompanied her life after Jake passed. She would continue to pray about her decisions and let God handle the outcome.

Summer breezes were pillowing the curtains at the kitchen sink window. Stephanie quickly finished pounding the bread dough and preparing it for the rising process. Making fresh rolls was a skill her own grandmother had drilled into her many years ago. Every time she made them, she reflected fondly on "Grandma's ways." Grandma Nancy would often pass along her takes on life. Memories of her were precious, and she often wished she would be able to pass along to her own children one day. Suddenly the phone jingled.

"Hello?" Stephanie inquired.

"Hi, Stephanie this is Mrs. Stevens from the library."

"Oh, hi. Nice to hear from you."

"Yes, well I have some good news to pass along. I hope," replied Mrs. Stevens. "The library board is interested in offering you the temporary position at the library for the summer while I have my knee replacement and recover at my daughter's place. Are you still interested?"

"Oh yes, I am," Stephanie replied enthusiastically.

"Well then, if you could find some time in the next few days and could come to the library, I will go over all the details with you. How about that?"

"Okay, yes. I will see you soon," Stephanie answered.

Hanging up the phone, Stephanie did a little jig around the room. A new job! She was feeling so grateful and delighted with the prospects and eager to fulfill an aspect of her college degree. Leaving the bread to rise, she went in search of John to share the good news.

4

John was mucking the soiled straw from one of the horses' stalls when Stephanie entered the barn.

"Hey, Dad, are you staying cool?" Stephanie inquired.

"Kind of hard to do on a one-hundred-degree day," replied John.

"Mrs. Stevens just called from the library, and she offered me the temporary position at the library. What do you think?"

John sensed the underlaying enthusiasm from Stephanie, and he wanted to support her in her dreams.

"I think that is a great opportunity for you, and one you shouldn't pass up. It may lead to bigger and better things for you as well."

"Well, I plan on going in to town and seeing her tomorrow, but I wanted you to know that I will still see to all my normal tasks."

"Oh, Stephanie, you have been a blessing to me ever since Jake introduced you to me and this farm. I would never want to hold you back from seeking a passion for working with children. We will continue as we always have working together to get it done." John chuckled.

Stephanie reached out and hugged John, smiling. "Thanks for your support. It means a lot to me."

Leaving John working in the barn, Stephanie returned to the house. She had to tell Trina about the call from Mrs. Stevens.

"Oh, I am so excited for you, and I hope it works for you," exclaimed Trina.

THE INHERITANCE

"Yes, me too. She mentioned coming to the library in the next few days to discuss the job. I am going to see her tomorrow," replied Stephanie.

Stephanie and Trina continued discussing the new job and the cute happenings of toddler Bobby. Sometimes Stephanie's heart ached to have what Trina and Brian shared. She wanted children desperately but quickly responded to the laughter and love in Trina's voice regarding little Bobby.

"How are your vegetables doing in this heat?" asked Trina.

"Well, it seems I have to water the beans and corn more frequently. The sprinkler system that John set up for me sure makes the job a lot easier," responded Stephanie. "I think I might go to the hardware store tomorrow and inquire about a timing system so when I am working at the library, John doesn't have to remember to water things as well. His plate is already full with managing the ranch and farm."

"That sounds interesting. I think Brian's friend Steve set up something similar for his wife last week," replied Trina.

Ending their conversation, Stephanie prepared to finish rolling out the bread dough. It had risen nicely in the warm environment.

Dinner tonight would involve some smothered steak and vegetables with the warm bread as a side. Stephanie continued preparing the evening meal, pondering on what her new job might be like.

* * * * *

Later that evening, when John came in for supper, he and Stephanie enjoyed the delicious supper and began a discussion on how they would manage the farm while she was working.

"I don't want to put unnecessary stress on you, John, with accepting this new job."

"Daughter, I told you earlier that I am pleased with this opportunity you've been given. I want you to enjoy it and not worry about things here."

"Well, I was talking with Trina earlier and mentioned to her that I wanted to look into a timer system for the sprinkler so that the vegetables would be watered. Do you think that is something worth looking into?"

"I will check with Tim at the hardware store tomorrow and see what is involved. I need to go get some bolts and nuts to finish a squeaky gate into the pasture."

"Oh, do you think we could ride into town together tomorrow? I mentioned to Mrs. Stevens that I would stop by and get information on the new job. I am not sure how long that will take."

"I think we could manage that. I need to go see Greg at the bank as well. The upcoming hay and wheat harvests will give us a nice bonus to add to our account at the bank."

John did not like to worry Stephanie about the money side of running a ranch and farm. He had done very well over the years, establishing credit and accumulating a hefty bank savings as well. There was always worry that equipment would need to be replaced or a roof needed repair so that is where having a nice credit standing benefited John when running the ranch. He was not always interested in paying the bills and managing the expenses however. He preferred being out in the fields or tending to the livestock.

Later, as Stephanie cleaned up the dinner dishes, John managed to sit at the desk and go through the mail. He noticed a flyer in the mail announcing the approaching opening of the new vet clinic and hospital. A picture of his son Justin was also on the page. He had not changed much over the years. His hair was still the irritant wave of brown matching the color of his. The smile on Justin's face indicated his excitement for this new venture. John just wished with his whole heart that he and Justin could resolve their discord.

As Stephanie entered the living room, she noticed John studying the flyer. She had looked at it earlier when bringing in the mail. Once again, she allowed her plan to take shape in her mind. Something needed to take place between Justin and his father. She just hoped the good Lord would help her out in making that happen.

5

The following morning John and Stephanie got in the truck to head into town, about fifteen miles up the road. Braintenburg was a bustling town of about five thousand. It was quickly growing since the new factory was opening soon. Now the new vet clinic and hospital also doted the horizon. It was located on the far side of town and therefore not right on the path that John and Stephanie took into town. A giant sign hanging near the highway invited patrons and the surrounding community to the upcoming celebration of the town's founding. This time was always an event that brought a huge crowd to town. Craft booths, food vendors, contests, and even a small carnival for the kids was planned to be held in about three weeks. Several of the community's churches also got involved with the invitation to attend a community service and enjoy fellowship with neighbors and friends.

"Looks like the town is bustling today," remarked John as he pulled to a stop in front of the town's two-story library.

"I should be no more than a couple of hours, I think," Stephanie replied. "Mrs. Stevens wanted to acclimate me to the computer system and explain how to check out books."

"No rush. I am going over to the feed store to check on delivery of my order and then plan to go shoot the bull with Tim down at the hardware store. I will look into the sprinkler system and get the necessary hardware to fix the gate. Just give me a call when you are ready."

Stephanie nervously climbed the steps to the imposing doors of the library. She was an avid reader herself and had made sure to get a library card last summer when she moved to the area. Coming here was nothing new to her. It was just now that she was going to be working here that it gave her an all-new, exciting feeling.

The doors squeaked softly as Stephanie entered the building. Straight in front of her was the wraparound desk for check out and where the librarian sat to monitor all the incoming patrons and others making use of the library's facilities.

"Good morning," announced Mrs. Stevens. "You have chosen an excellent time to come in today. We just opened thirty minutes ago, and it is still quiet in here. Come on around the corner of the desk, and we can get acquainted.

Mrs. Stevens was a short and heavyset woman with a head of gray hair and a welcoming smile.

Stephanie longingly looked around the area as if seeing it for the first time. *I guess from this view, it was the first time*, Stephanie decided.

Pulling up a chair next to Mrs. Stevens, Stephanie sat down.

"Oh, I am so relieved that the library will be in the hands of a young and promising lady. I have worked here for going on thirty years, and each day brings new adventures to me. Children coming in with their parents and story hour are two of my favorite events here at the library." Mrs. Stevens went on, "I know you are John Wilkes's daughter-in-law, but tell me more about yourself."

"Well, I am so thankful for this opportunity to do something I love, enjoying reading," Stephanie replied. "As you know, I obtained my teaching degree last spring and then married Jake Wilkes over the summer. Sadly, he passed away in December, leaving me to contemplate returning to my hometown or staying on with John. He has been so kind, and I have truly appreciated his sharing of our sorrow. He encouraged me to stay and come check out this position when Trina mentioned that you were having surgery."

"Yes, it is time for me to give in and get this sore knee replaced. Walking around the library reshelving books has taken its toll on these old knees. Well, let's get you introduced to the library and its fascinating functions."

THE INHERITANCE

For the next hour, Mrs. Stevens showed Stephanie how to run the computer system and the electronic way to check out new books. Most all the patrons of the library were exceptional about turning in books on time. She explained how to search and place requests that certain patrons had when requesting a certain book. Then they walked around the library, and she commented about each section. The adult section was located on one side of the library, and a another semidecorated area was designated the children's area on the other. There were conference rooms in the back and also lower level that were booked by certain committees in town for their use. The community club met here on the second Tuesday of each month at 6:00 p.m. Literacy classes were offered by tutors and given a special room to work in offering a little privacy as well.

"I am due to have my surgery a week from Wednesday, so if you could start tomorrow, that would be great. I will stay through till Friday and make sure you don't have any questions. Of course, you can feel free to give me a call if there are any issues that arise during my absence, but I am sure you will handle things nicely."

"Okay, I can manage that," Stephanie replied.

Ending their conversation and the brief tour, they arranged for a time that Stephanie could arrive tomorrow and the hours she would work.

Stephanie called John and told him she would be ready when he was able to arrive.

Twenty minutes later John pulled up to the library, and Stephanie hopped into the truck. John shared that he was able to obtain a timer for the sprinkler system, and Stephanie shared her news about the library.

When they arrived home, Stephanie went in to prepare some sandwiches for lunch while John worked on the timer system for the garden. New possibilities were beginning, and Stephanie felt her heart start to heal.

6

The next morning Stephanie left to go to the library, and John began his normal duties. He had hired on two of the young high school boys to assist him at least over the summer, and they were due to arrive at eight. He hoped they would work out and would show some enthusiasm and interest in the job.

A slight breeze rounded the corner of the house as John stopped to check on the timer system for the garden. Watering during the cool morning hours was important to keep the plants from withering in the hot sun and keep the ground moist and not hard and cracked.

The boys Tim and Justin arrived and appeared excited to begin their new jobs. John took them on a tour of the barns and stables. It certainly helped that both boys had at least a minor knowledge of the equipment and animals. They both were taking a course on farm management and belonged to the local FFA organization. Although neither boy lived on a farm themselves, they were grateful for the opportunity to gain some knowledge and experience that would look good on college applications if needed.

The first task of the day was to lay some fresh straw in the stables and feed the livestock. Handling the heavy bales was a definite reprieve for John as he showed them how to use the lift system to lower the bales from the hayloft to the ground, which made it easier to break apart and scatter in the stalls.

Showing them the mechanics of running a tractor and wagon was a definite trial. Pushing on the clutch and releasing the brake to move forward was an entertaining prospect. At first, the tractor jerked and sputtered to a stop when not enough pressure and release

THE INHERITANCE

was applied. Eventually, John managed to get the boys familiar with the running of the tractor.

John didn't want to overwork the boys and cause them to quit after the first day. The boys seemed to enjoy everything they were experiencing however. They were definitely hard workers, and John appreciated their enthusiasm and felt a sense of elation over sharing his life's work.

They stopped for lunch. John had sandwiches and chips to share with the boys. He mentioned that for the future they would need to bring their lunch from home. Once they learned the running of the farm, he planned to get caught up on bookwork and animal vaccinations so they would be on their own for the most part. He promised them an hour lunch or longer if they needed it. He was more about getting the job done than watching the clock. They seemed accepting of the laid-back experiences and promised to do their best for him.

* * * * *

At the library, Stephanie and Mrs. Stevens developed a good working relationship. While Mrs. Stevens checked in books, Stephanie located their position on the shelves. The library was a busy place as several locals came in to chat with Mrs. Stevens or check out the newest book release. Stephanie was excited to begin her new job and even had some lingering thoughts for interesting book displays. Of course, she realized that she was only temporary help, but she also wanted to make sure the library board recognized her efforts.

On Friday afternoon, Mrs. Stevens looked longingly around the library as if to stamp the memories in her mind. Stephanie realized it was hard for Mrs. Stevens to say goodbye, albeit only for a few weeks.

With a quiver in her voice, Mrs. Stevens said, "I know I am leaving the library in excellent care. I am just going to miss coming here every day. My daughter lives in Denbrooke, about an hour away. Please feel free to give me a call if anything comes up, and I will be happy to assist you."

"Of course, Mrs. Stevens. I will email you a progress report weekly if you would like."

With a final wave, she walked out of the library. Stephanie had the keys now, and it was her responsibility to look over all the areas and lock up. Stephanie prepared to complete her checkoff and headed home for the evening.

7

The following Monday, as Stephanie was unlocking the doors to the library, Mr. Jackson came running across the town square.

"Oh, Mrs. Wilkes, Mrs. Wilkes," he eagerly attempted to get her attention.

Mr. Jackson was the head of the library board, so Stephanie waited patiently for him to climb the steps. She knew she needed to address his immediate concerns.

"Good morning, Mr. Jackson. How can I help you?" Stephanie smiled and shifted her bag to her shoulder.

"Let's go on in," Mr. Jackson replied.

Lights were turned on, and Stephanie went on around to the back of the circular desk and waited for Mr. Jackson to address why he came to see her.

"I trust you are adjusting to the new position here?" inquired Mr. Jackson.

"Yes, I am eager to start on my own today," Stephanie answered. "Mrs. Stevens was extremely helpful last week, and I feel I am in a good position to give the library my full attention."

"Good, good. Well, the reason I am here this morning has to do with the Founding Days that will be here in about two weeks. You see the library has sufficiently managed to hold its own for a number of years, and we like it that way. However, the board has decided, with a new young woman in charge, it was time to make the library's presence in the town more noticeable. Are you following me, Mrs. Wilkes?"

"Yes, I think so, Mr. Jackson. But please call me Stephanie. What is it you were hoping to accomplish?"

"Well, the town council has agreed to a booth and possibly some lawn games to engage the children. It would also be an opportunity to display some books or talk about the programs the library has to offer. We, that is the library board, along with the town council, of course, are encouraging you to organize these thoughts and present a plan to us for approval by tomorrow night's council meeting."

Noticing the alarmed look on Stephanie's face, Mr. Jackson continued with his comments.

"Now do not feel that we expect a huge display. We know this is your first full day here, and you are probably already a little nervous, but we have every confidence in your abilities. We had discussed this possibility with Mrs. Stevens several months ago but had not heard back from her, and so we wanted to see if she had mentioned anything to you."

Finally, Stephanie worked up enough courage to answer Mr. Jackson.

"I appreciate your faith in me. I do have some ideas of my own for the library, but Mrs. Stevens did not mention anything to me about preparing for the town's Founding Days."

"I know she was in a lot of discomfort with her knees, and her mind was probably on the upcoming surgery and all of the worries with that," answered Mr. Jackson. "Well, the town council meets tomorrow evening in the lower level, and the library board has a spot on the agenda, so please work this over in your mind over the next two days, and I will check in with you tomorrow afternoon. Now I need to get back to my offices. Have a great first day, Mrs., er, Stephanie," Mr. Jackson finished with a smile before hurriedly exiting the library.

Stephanie was left standing in astonishment over what she had just been given as an assignment. How was she to plan for an event she was not familiar with at all and, more importantly, given such a large task almost as a test to her abilities to hold this position? Well, her first day was looking to be a tad bit overwhelming.

THE INHERITANCE

She quickly turned on the computers, finished turning on all the lights, and made a quick perusal of the library's areas. Then she quickly picked up her phone and called Trina.

When Trina answered, Stephanie quickly filled her in on everything Mr. Jackson had told her.

"How am I to plan for a booth at the Founding Days festival, and I have never attended one?" she implored of Trina.

The festival occurred at the end of July, coinciding with fireworks festivities, and she and Jake had married in late August. The town celebrated their Fourth of July festivities two weeks after the calendar date so as to extend the holiday in people's minds. Children always enjoyed an additional fireworks display.

"I am coming to town in a bit to complete some errands. I will stop by the library, and we can talk things over a bit, okay?"

Her friend's words calmed Stephanie's anxieties a bit as she prepared to begin her first day on the job. She needed to plan a children's book to read for Story Hour later in the week. Copies of some new releases were due to arrive in the mail today, and she needed to process them and get them quickly on display. Also, she could take the time to look up festival booths and see what was involved in that endeavor. Well, her first day certainly looked to be a memorable event.

Time quickly passed, and before she knew it, Trina was coming in to the library with Bobby on her hip.

"Oh, I am happy to see you," Stephanie announced.

"Anything to help my friend. I am excited for you and this new position. Together, maybe we can brainstorm some ideas," Trina announced eagerly.

Trina filled her in on what events were a part of the Founding Days festival. She mentioned that several flea markets set up tables. The local church ladies had a food booth. The school always planned events like singing and talent competitions on the bandstand. The town council encouraged all local citizen groups to find a way to get involved.

"It seems Mr. Jackson and the library board have joined in on this year's festivities. The library has not participated before. Probably because it would have been a bit overwhelming for Mrs. Stevens to plan and organize. Of course, she has been a great librarian, and the town loves her, but the library has just existed, you know, and not really been given any special recognition until now. Look at it this way, Stephanie, the library board feels confident in you and sees this as an opportunity to encourage the use of the library more," finished Trina.

Stephanie exhaled slowly and nodded in recognition of Trina's encouraging words. She proceeded to ponder some ideas in her head while Trina gathered Bobby's toys and laid them around him on the blanket to keep his attention.

"What about a lemonade booth?" inquired Stephanie. "We could use some library volunteers to serve lemonade and possibly cookies. Is it acceptable to charge a small fee for that as a way of generating some extra funds for future library projects? There could be a ring toss or lawn darts set up to draw kids to the booth."

"Now you are thinking," replied Trina excitedly.

For the next hour, Trina and Stephanie scribbled down some ideas to pass along to Mr. Jackson when he came in tomorrow afternoon. Then Trina needed to head home as Bobby was getting cranky and ready for his afternoon nap.

"Thank you very much, friend. You have calmed my anxieties a lot by coming to my rescue today," she replied as she said goodbye to her friend.

The rest of her day passed uneventfully as she checked out books and made recommendations for several library patrons.

Later that evening at dinner, she relayed her first-day memorable events to John. He listened intently before commenting.

"Ken Jackson has always found a way to stir up people. Most of the time in a good way, but there have been a few times that have leaned the other way. I guess, as a lawyer, he has a certain flair for convincing people to agree to things," John commented.

"Well, Trina and I have a list of ideas to present to him tomorrow. I guess, we will see how accepting he is to them."

8

The next morning, as Stephanie opened the doors to the library, a frantic Ken Jackson approached her.

"You know tonight is the council meeting, right, Mrs. Wilkes?"

"Stephanie, please. And yes, I do. It begins at 6:00 p.m., correct?"

Mr. Jackson seemed taken aback by Stephanie's confident reply.

"I have some ideas to present to the board tonight for the upcoming Founders Day celebration."

"Well then, that is very good," replied Mr. Jackson as he quickly retreated down the steps back to his office.

Shrugging off the strange approach, Stephanie quickly began her day. First, she sorted the returns for placing them back on the shelves. Then she checked her computer for incoming requests and delivery. Stephanie's back was to the door as she was gathering a stack of books off the return cart. The door opened, and a man approached the desk.

"Excuse me."

Stephanie quickly turned around with a smile and was taken by surprise. The shock must have shown on her face.

The man seemed surprised as well.

Silence hung in the air as the two looked questioningly at each other. A singe of electricity seemed to fill the air.

"I am sorry, but is Mrs. Stevens here today?" the man finally inquired.

Stephanie was momentarily frozen in her spot but quickly recovered. Maybe he didn't recognize her.

"Huh, no, she is not. Mrs. Stevens is out on medical leave, and I am the new librarian for at least the next four to six weeks. Is there something I can help you with?"

Again, the man looked questionably at her.

"She recommended a series of books to me, and I am in to get the next book in the series," the man replied.

"Oh well, maybe I can help you. What series are you reading?"

"I have or, huh, I am reading the Heroes of Quantico series," he stumbled. "The first book is called *Against All Odds*. I was hoping to get the second book *An Eye for an Eye*." He paused and then asked, "You look familiar to me. Do I know you?"

Stephanie was hesitant to begin this dialogue, but this was what she had asked in her prayers, so she said, "I think maybe you do. I am Stephanie Wilkes."

The recognition instantly appeared on his face. "Well," he remarked, "I guess you know that I am Justin Wilkes then."

Stephanie had seen pictures of her long-lost brother-in-law but was surprised to see him in the library. This is what she wanted though a chance to figure out a way to bring John and his son back together, so she knew she had to approach this very carefully.

"Mrs. Stevens left last week to get a knee replacement, and I was available and looking for some part-time work, so the library board has given me this opportunity," she explained. "I have seen your picture on the news and on some fliers around town. You are one of the new veterinarians at the facility they are building on the west side of town, yes?"

"Yes, I am."

"I am so very sorry to have heard of my brother's passing. As you know I, uh, wasn't welcome at the farm. And I had lost touch with Jake. So I didn't know how to pass along my condolences to you. Stephanie…may I call you Stephanie?" At her nod, he continued, "Do you think maybe we could talk sometime? I don't mean to interrupt your work right now."

Stephanie continued to stand in one spot and finally remarked, "Yes, I would like that. Let me see if we have the second book in that series you are wanting."

THE INHERITANCE

She moved to the computer and sat down, quickly typing in the name of the novel she was searching for.

"Yes, we do have it in now. I am surprised that we do. That series is a popular one, so maybe you should grab it now."

"Okay," Justin remarked. "I remember where the books were, so I will go get it. Thank you." He continued to look interestingly at her as he moved to go retrieve the book from the shelf.

After he moved away, Stephanie released a nervous breath. Wow, this was proving to be an interesting day. Part of her was nervous at finally meeting Justin. Another part of her was concerned. What would John think when she told him? Maybe she shouldn't just yet until she had an opportunity to talk with Justin. She was still speculating when Justin returned with the second book to check out.

"I know this must be a little nerve-racking for you as well as me," Justin remarked. "I just want to visit with you soon. I will be living in the area, and I think it might be time to mend fences, so to speak."

Stephanie nodded quickly agreeing to his comment. "Yes, I would welcome the chance to know you better."

"Can I ask a favor of you?" Justin asked.

"Yes," Stephanie replied.

"Can you not mention that you have spoken with me to my father just yet? I would like to explain my absence and my side first."

"Yes, I think I can do that. There is not much I don't tell John. He has been like my own father to me since Jake has been gone, and we share a special bond."

"I understand that. I just want to start slow in this process, and I feel that maybe this is a chance to do that. I am not sure either."

They agreed to meeting the next day over Stephanie's lunch break. She decided that that would be a beginning, and for the time being, she would keep this introduction all to herself. After all, meeting to talk things over was a beginning and one she was as curious to understand as anyone else.

* * * * *

Back on the farm the hired hands were helping John unload some hay in the hot sun. Suddenly, John became dizzy and needed to sit down. The two boys were concerned.

"Mr. Wilkes, are you okay?" one of the boys asked.

"Sure, just a little hot out here today," John muttered, trying to distract them from his episode and wanting the hay unloaded quickly so they could call it a day.

John knew there was more to his little episode than a dizzy spell, but he just wanted to be able to go in the house and rest for a few minutes, so he let the boys finish the unloading of the hay and dismissed them for the day. Stephanie was going to be late today anyway as she had to meet with the town council and library board that evening at six. It would give him some time to get cleaned up and relax for a few hours before she got home. He didn't want to worry her.

Slowly, he made it to the house and sat down at the kitchen table. His heart had been racing more lately, and he knew he should make an appointment with the doctor, but he was hesitant to do so for fear they would tell him what he feared—his heart was failing him!

He knew it was important to maintain good health. He was never one that willingly went to the doctor, but lately, he felt that it was becoming necessary. Maybe it wouldn't be such a big deal. He just needed to get it over with. He reached for the phone.

"Dr. Marcus's office," the receptionist answered. "How may I help you today?"

"Hello, this is John Wilkes. I was wondering if I could possibly make an appointment to see the doctor?"

"Well, actually I just had a cancellation for tomorrow at two. Would that work for you, John?"

"Yes, I can manage that," John replied.

It seemed that once again the Lord was helping him deal with all his concerns.

They continued to exchange information, and reluctantly, John hung up the phone and sighed. He sincerely wished he didn't need this appointment, but he also knew the problem needed to be

THE INHERITANCE

addressed. He decided that he wouldn't mention this to Stephanie just yet. He wanted to see if there was any cause for concern first.

* * * * *

That evening, as the town council prepared to commence their meeting, Stephanie waited nervously with Ken Jackson and Susan Phillips, the leaders of the library board, for their turn on the agenda.

"The meeting of the town council will begin now at 6:02 p.m. on Tuesday, July 15," remarked the mayor.

As beginning meeting formalities were attended to, Stephanie felt her nerves start to calm. She could do this. After all, if she wanted to have her own classroom one day, she would need to appear confident and knowledgeable. She had met with Ken and Susan prior to the start of the meeting and shared her ideas with them. They had both agreed that her ideas held merit and hoped that the town council would agree.

Finally, it was their turn. Ken Jackson addressed the town council and introduced Stephanie as the interim librarian taking the place of Mrs. Stevens, who was out for knee surgery.

Stephanie began her presentation.

"Good evening, I would like to say that given this opportunity to serve as the town's librarian for a brief while has been wonderful. As far as the upcoming Founders Day celebration my, our objective is to bring the public more aware of what the library has to offer in the way of services. I hope to share my enthusiasm for reading with the kids and adults of this community. Therefore, we would like to have a lemonade stand and some lawn game activities for the children. A small fee would be charged for a tall refreshing glass of lemonade. Children and parents would be given the opportunity to purchase raffle tickets for some prizes like books or a Kindle. Also, parents could purchase a string of tickets to use on some nearby lawn games like the dart toss to pop the balloons, a ring toss, and a fishing game. This would generate some funds for the library to use toward offering some visiting programs and speakers or authors in the future. Thank you for your consideration."

MARIE MALONE

The town council members looked inquiringly at each other. Stephanie noticed a slight nod was given to the mayor, so he called for a vote to approve the agenda presented by the library board. All yay votes were given. Mr. Jackson and Mrs. Phillips congratulated Stephanie on her fine presentation. They exited the meeting quietly.

"I will assist you with rounding up some volunteers for the lemonade booth and children's games," volunteered Susan.

"Thank you very much. I will design and print some raffle tickets tomorrow," Stephanie said.

"I will purchase the Kindle and books for prizes with library funds as I am the interim treasurer that should work well. I will also see to some change for the booth," volunteered Mr. Jackson.

"We appreciate your willingness to organize these things for the library on such short notice," commented Susan Phillips.

As Stephanie walked quickly to her car, she felt an exhilaration in her step as the excitement of the upcoming event played through her mind. There was a lot to see to yet, and she would be busy with planning over the upcoming days.

She quickly drove home and found John asleep in his recliner. It was a little after seven in the evening. *He must be tired from the day of baling*, Stephanie thought. She noticed he had warmed some leftovers in the microwave and proceeded to do so herself.

The noise awakened John.

"How did your meeting go?" he asked.

"Oh, very well. The town council and library board were pleased with the proposals I presented, and we are going to proceed with the planning of a booth at the upcoming festival. I am excited to begin," Stephanie finished.

"That is great news!" John remarked.

They visited while Stephanie finished her dinner. John left out the part of his upcoming doctor's appointment, and Stephanie didn't mention meeting Justin either.

"Well, there is another hot day messing with hay tomorrow, so I think I will turn in for the night," John decided.

28

THE INHERITANCE

Stephanie finished cleaning up the dishes and worked on preparing a casserole for tomorrow night's dinner before heading to bed herself.

9

The next morning at the library, Stephanie worked on designing an attractive raffle ticket and printed out several copies to cut apart. She was busy working when the front door opened, and in walked Justin Wilkes.

"Good morning, or almost afternoon," he remarked with a smile.

"Hello." Stephanie returned his smile. "Kathy will be here shortly to sit at the desk while I take my lunch break, so if you would like to head out back there is a picnic table area there for us to meet. Try to grab the table under the shade tree," she offered.

Once Kathy arrived, Stephanie joined Justin out back.

"This area is very nice to sit at," Stephanie commented. "I take advantage of it daily."

Justin nervously began, "I know this must seem awkward for you to first meet me and then also agree to meeting with me. Please eat your lunch, and I will try not to drone on too long."

"No, I, uh, am open to hearing your story. I only know what little Jake shared with me. John has not been too forthcoming with information either. I guess four years is a long time to develop feelings. Please go on."

"Well, growing up on the farm-ranch wasn't always easy. Dad expected us to do chores around the farm, of course, without complaint. I knew that and willingly completed what was asked of me. I just wasn't into the farm scene. I liked taking care of the animals though. It seemed Jake was more into the farm side. And I liked taking care of the pets, cows, and horses. When Mom was diagnosed,

THE INHERITANCE

it was hard. I had a closer relationship with her than with Dad. It seemed she understood what I was feeling. I could often talk things over with her. When Jake left for college, Dad tried to generate more interest for me by forcing me to work side by side with him. I know he noticed that I preferred the company of animals over working on the equipment or whatever else was required work. We would grudgingly argue about what I was not doing correctly. Then I left for college as well, and Dad was forced to do the work on his own. I never thought too much about that. I guess, I was just ready to leave. Of course, Jake went home on the weekends and breaks and relieved Dad of some of the work. I preferred to stay on campus and study. Veterinary college looked promising to me. Then Mom passed, and the ultimatum was given. I tried to make Dad understand what I was interested in, but he wanted nothing to do with hearing it. Words were exchanged that I wish I could take back now. I left in an angry huff and returned to campus. Jake finished his studies, and we stayed in touch briefly. I don't think he understood my reluctance to take over the farm either. It was easier to go home with fellow students over break than to return home, and I guess it became a habit for me—looking for opportunities to work on campus to earn money for vet school and avoiding the conflict at home. I heard through a friend that Jake had met someone that following spring, but I made no effort to get in touch with him either. I guess you stayed on campus and finished your degree after Jake graduated?"

"Yes, I had two years left. Jake and I visited on the weekends when we could," Stephanie volunteered. "He mentioned having a brother but also said there was a definite discord between you."

"I had a semester to finish basic studies, and then I began my courses in veterinary medicine. Dad had paid ahead for our college tuitions but not for continuing my studies in veterinary medicine. That became my responsibility, so I needed to find work. I found a job where I could also work on my degree. So I stayed there for a while, and when I needed to do my residency, I accepted a position at a dairy farm in California. It worked out great. Mike, a fellow vet student, and Craig another vet, suggested we open a vet clinic of our own. Mike's uncle is Doc Stevens here in town, and Mike knew that he was looking to retire in a few years, so he approached him about buying the business. That is how we ended up building the vet clinic here. Someone needed to come here and see to the finishing touches, so I volunteered," Justin explained. "I know all of this information is a quick rundown of the past few years, but I have always felt that my father was not receptive to my career choice and was as hardheaded about that, as I have found myself to be at times. However, four years have passed, and now I feel that God has led me back here for a reason, and I want to see about fixing things with my father."

Stephanie nodded her agreement. "John works very hard on the ranch. I know there are times that it is almost too much for him to accomplish on his own. He has hired some high-school boys for the summer, and they appear to be working out well. It's only been a few days however. I have prayed about this reunion so to speak since we got the flyer in the mail and noticed your picture announcing the opening of the new facility. I am prepared to assist in this endeavor as much as I can. Approaching John about this meeting will be a start. I didn't mention our introductions to him yesterday, so later when I get home, I think I will see how he reacts. Do you agree?"

"Well, yes, I don't know any other way. I do not want you to feel as if you need to be a mediator. I also understand your loyalty to my father, and I don't want to place you in a poor standing with him either."

"Oh, John and I have an open understanding. When Jake passed six months ago, I was totally lost. John sat down with me and offered that I stay on the farm and we would work out our grief together. My family lives in Iowa, and I didn't know about returning there. I had started to develop a life here, and John gave me that opportunity to pursue it further. I am so grateful for his offer, and we have worked out a caring relationship. I do not like to see him so overworked on a daily basis. I think if I mention that you came in to the library and introduced yourself, that it would be a start."

"Okay. All I know and feel is that I want this rift between us resolved, and I am willing to take the first steps to see that happen."

"I will be in touch soon then."

THE INHERITANCE

They exchanged numbers, and Justin left thanking her for helping him in this way. Stephanie finished her lunch and sat quietly in the shade, contemplating how she would broach the conversation with John later. She felt in her heart that John wanted this as well, so she sent up a prayer that words would come and feelings would be resolved.

* * * * *

Across town John Wilkes parked his truck in front of the doctor's office. He was hoping that making this appointment was the right thing to do. He knew he needed to address these feelings of his heart racing. Something wasn't right, and perhaps the doctor could relieve some of the worry associated with these feelings.

He entered the reception area and checked in with the receptionist. She told him to take a seat and the nurse would call him back shortly to see the doctor.

About five minutes later, Carla, Dr. Marcus's registered nurse, appeared in the doorway.

"Hello, John, would you follow me, please?"

John got up and followed Carla down the long hallway to an exam room.

Carla began her part of the assessment. She took his blood pressure and measured his heart rate.

"It seems both measurements are a little on the high side today, John. What are you here to discuss with the doctor today?"

John knew Carla through a friend and was a little hesitant to share his concerns with a familiar person.

"Well, I felt it was time for a checkup, and umm, I also have been having a few chest pains and feel that, umm, my heart might be racing a little," he finished hesitantly.

"Okay, I will jot these things down, and the doctor should be in shortly. Just relax, John. We want the doctor to get accurate readings. Dr. Marcus is a wonderful doctor, and I feel confidently that he will address your concerns." She smiled, patted John on the hand, and left the exam room.

About two minutes later, Dr. Marcus entered.

"John! Nice to see you. It has been a while since I've seen you last. How have you been? Hay harvest is underway, I assume," he attempted to visit with John in an effort to relax him.

"Yes," John agreed. "It seems we pick the hottest days of the summer to bring in the hay."

"Yes, my dad and brother are working on the same thing right now. I am glad I have an air-conditioned office to work in right now."

John knew that Pete Marcus's ranch was across the valley on the opposite side of town. He also knew that his situation was similar to his own. He had three sons however, and two of them had chosen careers outside of the farming business.

Dr. Steve Marcus checked his notes and the readings for the blood pressure and heart rate.

"What are your concerns today, John?" he continued.

"It seems that my heart is beating wildly more than normal some days. I know the heat and hard work can bring on some of that, but it has caused me recently to be dizzy, and I guess, I just wanted to make sure that everything was still working," he finished on a chuckle.

"John, I wish I had a few more readings of your heart rate before I make an honest diagnosis. How would you feel about wearing a heart monitor for a few days? This would allow me to monitor your heart during different times of the day and also during times of strenuous work and relaxation times."

He continued before John could declare any hesitancy, "It is on a lanyard that fits around your neck and rests over your heart. It will need to be fastened to your chest area using these Velcro strips. Then a reading is sent via a program inside the device, and I will then ask you to return in three days, and we will see what needs to be done to address any issues. Are you willing to do this?"

John was listening, and while concerned with the appearance of such a device and using it, he decided he needed to do so, and hesitantly agreed.

After showing him how to place it and other instructions, John left the doctor's office and went on home. He knew he would have to explain to Stephanie and wanted to assure her it was just a preventive device and there was nothing to worry about.

10

Later that evening, when Stephanie came in, John had set the table for dinner and had placed the casserole in the oven per Stephanie's instructions from the morning. It was about done.

"How was your day?" they both started to say at the same time.

They chuckled, and Stephanie answered, "Fine. I had a lot occur at the library today."

She knew how imperative it was to tell John about Justin's visit and to approach it carefully. She certainly didn't want to upset John. She felt nervous but started the conversation.

"How about your day, John? Baling going, okay?"

John didn't want to put off talking with Stephanie any longer, so he replied, "Stephanie, can we sit down and talk a bit?"

"Sure, Dad. I always welcome a good conversation with you." Secretly, she was okay with putting off the part of her conversation for a few minutes.

"Stephanie, I do not want to alarm you in any way," he began and watched as Stephanie's eyes and face registered her questioning concern. "I went to the doctor today."

"Dad, what is wrong?" Stephanie asked in an alarming way.

"My heart has been giving me notice that something might be wrong. I felt it was only right that I go get a checkup, so I went to see Dr. Marcus this afternoon."

"Okay...and what did he say?"

"He has given me this heart monitor to wear around my neck for a few days." He stopped to show the device to Stephanie.

"Apparently, it will measure what my heart is doing throughout the day and record any quirks," he finished.

Releasing a sigh of acceptance, Stephanie checked over the device and nodded her approval.

"Well, it is important to make sure that everything is okay, John. And I am sure that if it shows any discrepancies that Dr. Marcus will know just what to do about it," she answered assuredly.

"Yes, I am sure as well. Dr. Marcus explained the workings of this thing. It will just be me getting used to wearing it for a few days, I reckon." He sighed as he finished, "Now how about your day? Anything of impending concern?"

Stephanie decided quickly that now was not the time to bring up meeting Justin. She really didn't want to keep things from John, but after hearing about the heart monitor and his hesitancy, she didn't want to contribute to the monitor recording inaccurate readings if hearing about Justin caused him any distress.

"Oh, it was a wild day with the children's hour and needing to read my first book to a bunch of antsy four- to six-year-olds. I had chosen an *Amelia Bedelia* book and wasn't sure the kids would catch the mixed-up words, but they chuckled at some of her silly misunderstandings, and it also gave me the chance to feel that I was teaching as well," she hurriedly finished, hoping John bought into her explanation.

This was going to be tough for Stephanie. She knew that Justin was wanting closure to the rift between him and his father. Yet another part of her was certain that John also wanted to fix things with his son but was now the right time. Should she reveal what she knew? She hated feeling caught in the middle, but that is just what she was—caught. She eventually decided to steer the conversation in another direction and asked how the two hired boys were coming along.

"They are working out well thankfully. They take the heavy lifting away. I can give them a job or two to do, and it is getting done. Maybe not exactly the way I would do it, but it is satisfactory for now, and they will learn as time goes on," John replied.

THE INHERITANCE

Dinner ended, and John retired to the family room to read the days mail and watch some news on TV. Stephanie cleared the table and started doing the dishes. She felt such angst over the current situation. Talking with Justin today had revealed a side she could relate to. Her parents didn't understand why she had to go so far away to college. She remembered her father questioning her repeatedly. Was a teaching career what she really wanted to do? Eventually, they supported her decision, but there were several times she sensed that her parents wanted her to choose something differently. She hadn't liked the feeling of discord between them. Then when she had told them about meeting Jake and getting married, it sealed the deal to the fact that she wouldn't be returning back home as another feeling of letdown entered the picture. They managed to come to the small wedding and had taken a liking to Jake. They had remarked about the beauty of the ranch and didn't understand again why she wouldn't be accepting a position in teaching immediately. So, yes, she understood how a parents approval affected your choices. In the end, God's plan was for her to stay in Montana, and now she was beginning to understand a lot more. She would have to talk with Justin soon and explain about her hesitancy in revealing his appearance. She knew he would be eager to hear how her evening had gone, and she had to convince him to be patient and understand.

* * * * *

The following morning Stephanie was working on cataloging some books and making some notes about the upcoming festival when Justin entered the quiet library.

She could tell by the questioning look on his face that he wanted to know about how telling John had gone.

"Good morning, Stephanie," he started.

"Good morning, Justin," Stephanie answered in return.

"So once again I have managed to interrupt your work day. I just couldn't wait to hear how things went telling my father, and I had to come see you."

"I understand fully, Justin. Let me explain. First, do not be alarmed, but I did not reveal our meeting to John yet. When I got home last night, John surprised me by telling me he went to the doctor yesterday about a possible heart problem." Noticing the alarmed and quirky tilt to Justin's head, she continued, "I was hesitant to mention our meeting after he revealed that he was to wear a heart monitor for a few days to record any missed beats of his heart. I was unsure about how telling him might contribute to a misrecording. So I made a rather hasty decision not to say anything just yet. Do you understand?"

"Wow, how is he doing? I was unaware of any health problems he might be experiencing. Of course, I wouldn't have known that, I guess."

"I just felt that we needed to wait at least a few days until the doctor could possibly see what was causing John's heart irregularities. I know how important fixing this rift is to you, but can you please see my point in waiting?"

"Yes, yes, I, uh, do get that," he stumbled over his answer, registering his concern for his father and his disappointment in not starting the reunion process.

"I will keep you updated, Justin, at least as much as I know when I know, okay? I really want this resolved for you both. I genuinely feel that John is ready and willing to talk with you as well. He saw the flyer the other day about the grand opening of the clinic, and I could see the expression on his face and believe that he wants this too," Stephanie remarked.

"I am so sorry to put you in the middle of what must feel like a heavy weight for you. I do appreciate your willingness to help in this endeavor, and I do understand. I will check back with you in a few days then," he finished and turned to leave the library.

At that moment, the phone rang, and Stephanie grabbed it as Justin left through the front doors, shoulders sagging.

"Hello, this is the library, Stephanie speaking," she answered.

After addressing the patron's concern, Stephanie sat at her desk and pondered the situation. Maybe she should just tell John about meeting Justin. Then she would know what kind of obstacles were

THE INHERITANCE

in her path. She felt that Justin had a deep desire to right things with his dad, and if she could help in that, she wanted to. Right now she needed to finish the final tasks to prepare for the upcoming festival in five days.

*****

At the end of the day Stephanie closed the library doors and locked them before walking to her car. The sun was a warm reprieve after the coolness of the library. The drive home was a relaxing trip, and as she pulled into the drive, she noticed that John was leaning on the fence staring at the hillsides.

She quietly closed the car door and walked over to the fence where John was standing. He didn't hear her walking up to him and appeared startled when he realized she was standing next to him.

"You were in deep thought," Stephanie commented.

"Oh, you know I just have a lot of things on my mind," John replied.

"Want to share? I am a good listener."

"You are sweet for asking. I do not know how I could have survived without your companionship and love. I truly enjoy having you here with me on the farm. I am so thankful that you decided to stay. Now you have a wonderful job that appears to satisfy you, and I sense that you are releasing some of your grief."

"Yes, I am enjoying working at the library. There are so many things that I would like to attempt there. However, I know I am just temporary, so most of the time I have to talk myself out of the notion to make changes. I miss Jake as well. I know he would expect me to continue on even on the tough days. I have to remind myself of that. He was a great husband and son. I will always hold a special place in my heart for the short time we got to spend together."

With tears in his eyes, John replied, "I know, Stephanie. He was a great son, and there were so many things we talked over about changes we wanted to start here on the farm as well. I must force myself to continue on." He sighed as he turned from admiring the view.

Was now the time to bring up the mention of Justin? Should she inquire about his thoughts about Justin? It seemed that John was done reminiscing for the moment, and the chance passed without resolution.

At the dinner table, Stephanie asked about the monitor that he was wearing and about the tasks he had completed during the day.

He told her that the monitor was hardly noticeable and that for the most part the two hired boys were completing the heavy tasks. They were working out well, and he enjoyed the assistance they provided. He also mentioned that he would be going to the doctor next Monday and was anxious to hear what the monitor had recorded.

They left the table and retired to the living room to listen to the news for the day. The weather appeared to be stabilizing for the next seven days, which was good news to Stephanie. She certainly hoped for calm warm days for the upcoming festival.

* * * * *

Over the weekend, Stephanie worked in her garden and watered the flowers around the porch. She planned the meals for the next several days as well. She knew that from Wednesday to Saturday John would have to fend for himself, so to speak, and she wanted to make sure he had plenty of leftovers to choose from.

Saturday afternoon, as she was sitting on the porch, Trina and toddler Bobby came riding up the road on a bicycle. She was always happy to see her friend and welcomed them up to the porch for a cool drink.

"Bobby was getting antsy in the house, and the only way I could think of entertaining him was to get on this bike and ride. It also is forcing me to get some exercise, as if running after Bobby isn't enough!" Trina chuckled.

"Well, I for one am happy to see you both today. I just finished watering the flowers and was taking a break to ponder on meals to fix for next week," Stephanie remarked.

"How are the plans for the festival coming along?" Trina inquired.

THE INHERITANCE

"Very well. We have volunteers lined up to serve lemonade and monitor the children's activities. Ken Jackson, Susan Phillips, and I will be selling raffle tickets for a chance to win some prizes. It appears that it will be a success. The weather is looking promising, and even though I have never attended such a festival here, I feel the enthusiasm will pay off."

"Brian, Bobby, and I plan to come into town each day. Brian says the petting zoo is to be assembled, and that will delight Bobby, I am sure. Mrs. King always has a beautiful display of rugs, blankets, and towels that depict her skills in sewing. I enjoy looking over all those choices. Brian says that the tractor and truck pull will bring a large crowd from the surrounding towns. I haven't always attended that part in the past. The loud noises scared Bobby the first year we went. So I leave that event for Brian to enjoy. The church dinners are always delicious as well. Maybe, John could come in for those, and you wouldn't have to worry about fixing some meals."

"I asked him about that," Stephanie remarked. "He says he prefers to avoid the large crowds this year. The memories of participating with Jake in the tractor pull are still too fresh for him to handle."

"Well, I understand that as well," Trina remarked. "They offer to-go containers, and I wouldn't mind picking one up for him and bringing it to the farm."

"I will ask him. It is so kind of you to offer. I just know with having this new position of librarian I should be available at the booth. We are hoping to sign people up for library cards and want to advertise other services we offer at the library that I am not sure people realize we offer."

"Let me know if I can help in that way. I guess we need to be on our way. It seems Bobby is getting antsy again."

The toddler was running around on the porch and stomping his feet as he noticed the cattle approaching in the field.

As they prepared to leave, Stephanie found herself wishing she could share with Trina her dilemmas with wanting Justin and his father to resolve their conflicts. She just needed someone to talk things over with. Yet she knew she wanted this reunion to work out, and if she could tread carefully and not alert John to anything, that would be best for now. She fully trusted Trina with anything, but she knew asking her not to mention anything to Brian and so forth just compounded the secrets.

"See you at church tomorrow." She waved as the two took off down the lane toward home.

11

Sunday's sermon was on forgiveness. Stephanie marveled at the Lord's work in bringing this message on this particular Sunday. She watched John's face as the sermon progressed. She hoped the message was entering his mind and heart. After several beautiful hymns and prayers, the service ended. As they exited down the aisle, several people greeted them with smiles and handshakes.

Shaking Pastor Steve's hand, John inquired quietly to Pastor Steve if he could speak with him later in the week.

Sensing John's need for secrecy, he remarked quietly, "Sure, John, I'd welcome a visit anytime."

John nodded and continued on down the steps of the church.

Stephanie had noticed the quiet exchange between Pastor Steve and John but chose not to acknowledge it to respect John's privacy.

* * * * *

Later, as Stephanie finished preparing the fried chicken for dinner, she sent up a silent prayer that this might be a turning point for Justin and John's relationship. She too would have to be patient and let the Lord do his work in his time.

"Are you prepared for the festival this weekend?" John asked at dinner.

"Yes, I feel good about how all the volunteers at the library have agreed to assist in lemonade making and serving. We have several volunteers assisting with the children's games as well. I just hope it will be a success."

"It can't help but be since you are the organizer," John complimented. "This fried chicken is moist and delicious, Stephanie."

"Thank you," Stephanie replied. "Have you given any thought to Trina's offer to bring you some of the carry-outs from the church dinners?"

"Yes, and if Trina is willing, I will accept her offer. I just am not up for too much socializing, and we have to finish the hay harvest this week, so I think I will be ready to enjoy that by the end of the day."

"John, what day is your doctor's visit?"

"I have an appointment on Tuesday morning to check the results of the monitor's recordings, I guess. I still don't know how a small box can record the beatings of a heart."

"Modern medicine is a marvel indeed. I will be anxious to hear the results."

"Well, I've hardly noticed wearing this device. Only when I dress and undress, I realize it is there." John chuckled. "I am wondering what it has to say as well."

The rest of the Sunday afternoon passed as Stephanie relaxed by reading a novel she meant to finish and John studied the newspaper before taking a quiet nap in his recliner.

* * * * *

Monday morning arrived, and Stephanie entered the library with anticipation. This week would be busy, and she was looking forward to the final preparations for the festival. Children's Hour would still be held on Wednesday morning, and then in the afternoon, set up for the festival would begin in the park. She quickly began her normal duties for the day and was busy checking in a stack of books that had been returned over the weekend when the front doors opened and Justin walked in.

"Good morning, Stephanie."

"Hello, Justin."

"I felt I owed you an apology for the way I left here last week. I certainly do not mean to put you in the middle, as I explained. I

THE INHERITANCE

guess I have always experienced a bit of impatience. I have reached a point in my life where I want to right my wrongs and make peace with my father, if he is willing," Justin finished.

"Oh, I understand, Justin, I do. I want John to find some peace as well." She continued, "You want to know what I find enlightening? Yesterday's sermon at church was on forgiveness. I don't know what your faith involves, but I feel that the Lord had a hand in bringing that message at this time."

Justin answered with a slight grin. "I do believe, Stephanie. My parents were insistent on attending church and sent us to Sunday school weekly. I grew up with a strong faith. When I was in college, I attended services weekly at a small chapel on campus. Later, when I moved to California for my job, the foreman at the ranch invited me to attend services with him and his family. Oh, there were several Sundays that I did miss due to job responsibilities, but I continue to share in the comfort of God's word. I've only been back in this area a few weeks and haven't attended church yet. I guess a part of me was hesitant to come for fear of meeting up with my father there before we had a chance to reconcile, if you know what I mean."

"Well, I am not sure if you are aware but this coming Sunday is a service in the park. It is not a certain denomination but more of a praise service, I am told. This will be my first experience with attending the service as well. Jake and I were not yet married, and I was still at home last summer at this time. Perhaps you would like to check it out?"

"I did see the announcement pinned up at the feed store," Justin remarked. "I think having this service is something new for the town as I don't remember them offering it four years ago."

"John most likely will not attend the service," Stephanie explained. "He has mentioned earlier that a service outside of God's house was not something he was interested in. I am sure he will tune in to a service on the television Sunday. So if you are interested…"

"I will try to make it to the park sometime this weekend, and I will consider attending the service as well. Thanks for the invite and voice of encouragement," Justin finished.

45

"You are most welcome. Have a good week, Justin, and maybe I will see you around the park?"

"Yes, you as well, Stephanie." He turned to leave the library, then with a quick turn of his head to look back, he smiled quickly.

Well, that worked out well, Stephanie thought. Justin was a kind man, it seemed, and she wanted to continue to encourage the reconciliation of John and his son in any way that she was able.

Several library patrons came in to return books or check out new ones, so the library was a bustling place over the next few days. Stephanie continued to work on plans for the festival and felt good about the schedule she had established and the games that she prepared.

12

On Tuesday, John waited patiently and nervously to be called back to visit with the doctor. He had removed the device when he entered the office and now was waiting for them to print out results and time to consult with Dr. Marcus. It seemed the clock was moving slowly today.

"John?" Nurse Carla interrupted his wayward thoughts. "Dr. Marcus will see you now."

John followed her down to the exam room.

"You can sit there if it is more comfortable than the exam table," Carla remarked, indicating the arm chair next to the desk.

She continued by taking his blood pressure and measuring his heart rate. When she finished, she said that Dr. Marcus would be in shortly.

John waited about five minutes before Steve Marcus entered the exam room.

"Good morning, John." He smiled as he entered the room.

"Morning, Doc," John replied.

"Let's get down to business and discuss these results from the monitor. It seems that your heart does tend to beat erratically from time to time and not necessarily at a certain time of the day or during what I assume to be more physical labor. There is really not a big concern about this. I would like to recommend some heart medicine that will help with regulating your heart rate. It does not mean that your heart is quitting or necessarily a cause for you to be concerned with an attack.

MARIE MALONE

"I would like to see you not do as much strenuous labor simply due to age and not the condition of your heart. The muscles of your heart sound good. We can do an EKG if you would and confirm that all the muscles are good. A stress test is always a good idea as well," he finished.

"What kind of pills and for how long?" John inquired.

"It is a pill you would take once a day preferably in the morning and most likely for the rest of your life, John. I am going to recommend that you schedule that EKG with my nurse just to make sure that all looks well too. You would do that test over at the hospital in Billings."

"Well, if you think that the pills would help, then I guess I will agree to that. As for the tests, now is not necessarily a good time to be taking off for Billings to do a test. So I would like to put that off for now."

"Well, John, I will prescribe the pills. But I will be on your case to get that test done before harvest. And I will want to see you in my office in two weeks to check your heart rate again."

"Oh, does this mean I have to wear that device some more?" John asked.

"Yes, until we are certain that the pills are doing their job, and as mentioned before you get that test scheduled to rule out any blockages, then I will be agreeable to getting rid of the device."

Upon hearing the word *blockages*, John nodded hesitantly and said he would check with Carla about scheduling the test. He certainly didn't want to think that a blockage might cause a heart attack in the future.

"Excellent, I am glad to hear that you are so agreeable," Steve Marcus commented.

After handing John the pamphlet about the EKG test and what it involved, Dr. Marcus went to the front desk with John.

"Carla, please schedule John for an EKG in another month." He looked to John for confirmation. "And an appointment to return to the office in another two weeks. Take care, John, and feel free to call the office if you have any more concerns." Dr. Marcus quietly returned down the hallway to see his next patient.

THE INHERITANCE

John finally left the office with his appointment reminder and Carla's assurances that she would call with the time for the EKG soon. She also reminded him to go by the pharmacy for his medicine.

"Well, at least I know now that the issue is not as bad as I anticipated," John told himself and felt better about the fact that taking a small pill might help him to feel more reassured. He would tell Stephanie later about his visit as he knew she would want to know everything the doctor had said.

Turning the truck to head for the pharmacy across town, he decided to drive by the construction site for the new veterinary clinic. "Just out of curiosity," he told himself.

The building appeared to be complete on the outside. They were even markings in the parking lot. It looked like the clinic would be opening on time. Of course, the insides were probably not finished John reminded himself. He wondered if his son would be waiting to come after the opening and would he make the effort to get in touch.

As he continued on to the pharmacy, John remembered that he wanted to stop in to visit with Pastor Steve. So after getting his medicine, John went by the church office.

Pastor Steve was in his office at the church. No one was in the front office. Sherilyn, the church secretary, must have gone to lunch. John knocked on the inner door.

"John! Come in, come in. Nice to see you!" said Pastor Steve with a welcoming smile.

"Am I interrupting your lunch or anything?" John asked.

"No, not at all. Sherilyn just stepped out to mail some letters, and I was looking at the plans for Sunday's service in the park. Come in and have a seat," directed Pastor Steve as he motioned to the small sofa in the corner. "What brings you by today? I am always happy to visit with parishioners."

"Well, Pastor, your message this past Sunday on forgiveness has got me thinking. I am not sure you know my whole story as you've only been with us as a pastor for about six months," John explained.

"John, I had just accepted the position here when your son Jake lost his life in the riding accident. I wanted to be there for you to console you and your daughter-in-law, Stephanie. And my mentor,

49

Pastor Mike, explained a few of the details. He only mentioned that you had another son, Justin, but did not go into any other details. Since then I have heard that you don't have any contact with Justin, and I have prayed many times for you and your family."

"Thank you for the prayers, Pastor. They are always appreciated." John hung his head and appeared to be contemplating his next words.

Pastor Steve just sat and waited patiently.

"I want to make amends with my son," John quickly voiced. "I don't know if you are aware, but the new vet clinic opening on the other side of town belongs to my son. I have seen several flyers and advertisements, and it has opened my eyes to the fact that Justin and I need to talk. I just don't know where to begin or how? Forgiveness is a hard pill to swallow."

"Yes," Pastor Steve agreed. "Forgiving someone and asking for forgiveness is a huge endeavor. God tells us in his Word that forgiveness is a powerful thing." He quoted 1 John 1:8–9. "If we claim to be without sin, we deceive ourselves and the truth is not in us. If we confess our sins, he is faithful and just and will forgive us our sins and purify us from all unrighteousness. I encourage you to read Psalms 25, 32, 38, and 51. They are encouraging psalms that are on sin and repentance."

After a few minutes of appearing to contemplate the pastor's words, John rose to leave and put forth his hand to shake.

"Thank you for your comforting words today, Pastor Steve. I will take everything into consideration and ask for your prayers while I do so."

"Of course, John," added Pastor Steve. "Will we see you at the community service on Sunday?"

"No, I prefer our small congregation, and this will give me time to study His Word at home. Have a nice day, Pastor." Then he turned to walk out.

On the short trip home, John thought back to the time when his sons were growing up. Deep down, he knew that Jake had the farming bug in him and Justin didn't. He remembered multiple times when Margorie would gently say to him to be patient with Justin and

THE INHERITANCE

accept his choices. While he heard what Margorie had said, the stubbornness in him demanded that he change the way Justin felt about the farm. He wanted to leave the farm in both of his sons' capable hands. He was proud of what his family legacy had given him to take care of, and he wanted his children to feel that same way. Now he had two young boys hired to work the farm, and his heart hurt for the chance to change that.

13

Stephanie was anxiously waiting for the volunteers to arrive with a truck to take some supplies to the park to be set up. Today would be a day for the whole festival committee to set up tables and check for needed supplies and enough electrical outlets to satisfy the needs of the booths and vendors. While she still wasn't sure truly what to expect from this festival, she had been told that it drew crowds from all the neighboring towns as far as one hundred miles away.

When the truck arrived, Stephanie helped to load the lemonade supplies and book displays that she wished to set up. She also had pamphlets advertising all the services of the library and how to apply for a library card. Adding the stack of applications to a box, she quickly locked the doors to the library. It would remain closed for the remainder of the week while the festival was going on. Her hours would definitely change over the next few days, but she was looking forward to this event.

Arriving at the park, she was surprised to see all the activity taking place. There were vans unloading displays and tables for their wares. Several of the local farmers she assumed were connecting panels together for the petting zoo. The bandstand was crowded with musicians from the high school setting up for their concert tomorrow evening. She had heard that several local bands were due to perform as well. A country music star who called his home in Billings was due to take the stage on Friday evening. She was certain that would bring a crowd to their town and festival as well. A food truck was attempting to park near the sidewalk and curb to draw hungry festivalgoers and current workers to taste their products. A large tent

THE INHERITANCE

was being assembled as a shade area to relieve patrons from the hot sun and a place to rest and enjoy the music performances. Later in the week, it would house the community service goers. She located the tent where the library would be serving lemonade and also offering the games for youngsters to enjoy.

"Hello, Mrs. Wilkes," replied Ken Jackson.

"I prefer Stephanie, please," she answered.

"Oh yes, Stephanie. As you can see, we have a large area designated for the games, and the tent area will be used for serving the lemonade and cookies. I will bring a cash box by tomorrow morning. If you need anything else, I am sure there will be a number of volunteers here to assist."

"Yes, I have the signup sheet here with me so that I know who will be coming and when."

"Well, it appears you will be just fine then. I will check in sometime tomorrow then. Have a good evening."

Stephanie quickly placed the boxes with the pamphlets and library card applications under the table. Making a note to bring a table cloth from home tomorrow, she left the booth and headed home.

* * * * *

Upon arriving home, Stephanie noticed the high-school workers preparing to leave for the day and John was talking to them under the large shady oak tree. He waved as she pulled into the drive.

Stephanie went on into the house and put her things on the counter before wandering over to check the Crock-Pot with tonight's dinner inside. It smelled delicious, and it looked as if it was ready to eat. She decided to quickly change her clothes, and then she planned to set the table for dinner. Later, she wanted to go check her vegetable garden as tonight might be the last time to check it for the next few days.

John sauntered into the kitchen just as Stephanie was finishing setting the table.

"Hi, Dad, how was your day today?" Stephanie inquired.

"Hot!" John chuckled and then continued, "It was a good day. I feel I made a good decision in the two boys I hired for the summer. They jump in and complete tasks without having to be told. They were just asking me about the possibility of taking off a few hours earlier tomorrow evening to head into town for the festival. I told them that would be fine and that I was pleased with their work efforts and that they deserved some fun time with their friends. I said we would take off at noon tomorrow as all the hay baling is caught up and wheat harvest is still a week away. They were definitely in a good mood when they left. How about your day, Stephanie?"

"It was all good as well. I went up to the festival grounds this afternoon to see about setup. There was definitely a lot of activity going on. Ken Jackson had our booth all ready to go, so there was not much for me to finish up there. I am looking forward to seeing the crowds tomorrow. It will be a new experience for me," Stephanie finished.

"Those days are long behind me, I think. We used to go to every festival around as a family. The boys used to enjoy running from one activity to another. Marge and I preferred the shade tent and visiting with folks," John reminisced, quietly appearing to be lost in thought for a moment.

"Have you changed your mind about coming to the festival at least to get some food and maybe see some neighbors for a bit?"

"Oh, Stephanie, I don't think so. Memories of Jake and I entering the calf roping, tractor-and-truck pulling, and crop exhibits are all still too fresh, I am afraid. I prefer to just relax here at home. Thanks for setting up meal delivery with Trina. She sent word that she will be bringing by some chicken and noodles tomorrow evening. I want you to enjoy this festival as it is your first in the town, and don't worry about me. I will be just fine here at home," John finished.

"Well, okay then. If I can't change your mind, I will be gone all day and into the early evenings, but you know how to reach me."

Later, Stephanie went out to the garden and noticed a fresh picking of green beans and gathered a few onions and radishes. Later in the month, she would anticipate some fresh sweet corn and other vegetables long into September, she hoped.

THE INHERITANCE

As she prepared for bed, she thought how anticipating this festival, and enjoying it with Jake would have been so enjoyable. She had been working hard on mental healing. She missed Jake a lot. Their love was still fresh in her mind. She enjoyed living here on the ranch with John, but a part of her also knew that couldn't last forever. She wanted to experience that new love and a fresh life again someday, but for now she was content to stay here and anticipate the future.

14

The next morning was bright, sunny, and warm. Stephanie finished baking her batch of cookies and bagging them in cellophane wrappers before she left for the festival. Meeting new people and watching the goings on of a festival put a smile on her face. She waved to John and the high-school boys before leaving.

The parking lot was filling already at 9:00 am, probably most of the festival workers, Stephanie decided. She grabbed her basket of cookies and the tablecloth she wanted to add to the festival booth and headed toward all the action. Ken Jackson and Rita, a volunteer, were just unveiling the tarp that covered the booth as she approached.

"Good morning!" Stephanie addressed the pair.

"Good morning, Mrs., er, Stephanie," Ken said. "I have the money box for change right here. I will check in with you throughout the day to see if there is anything else you might need, but best wishes. I hope all goes well." He quickly left the area.

"Well, it appears he was in rather a hurry this morning." Rita, a sixty-year-old volunteer, chuckled as she shook her head and finished setting up the chairs behind the booth's counter. "Of course, Ken Jackson never could sit still for long as a young child either. He was a student in my third-grade class a number of years ago."

Stephanie smiled as she added the decorative tablecloth to the booth.

"I know we have met at the library many times, and I am so appreciative of you volunteering this morning as this is the first day and my first day of this festival as well. You will be a valuable resource in the day's activities I am for sure," Stephanie added.

THE INHERITANCE

"I am always happy to volunteer for the library. I believe reading is the best gift you can encourage in young children and older adults as well. It is a gift that keeps on giving is my motto. So we will tackle this endeavor together. As you know, this booth idea is new for the festival, so I am anxious to see how it goes over as well. If we can convince a child to come check out the library, it will all be worth it. I do hope that you will have a chance to see more of the festival as well. We will figure out a way to make that happen," finished Rita.

The morning began slowly as not as many visitors were attending the festival just yet. School was due to dismiss for the long weekend at 1:00 p.m. Most farmers had morning chores to attend to, and unless you were retired, others had jobs to head to for the day.

Stephanie had secured a list of high-school volunteers to monitor the kids' games starting this afternoon. She knew most of them were eager to assist as a bonus credit for community engagement and service to add to their college applications and etc. She settled in and started to enjoy the festival coming to life. Wonderful aromas were beginning over by the food truck, and the women's group was setting up for this evening's chicken-and-noodle dinner to be served beginning at four. She knew Trina would be coming to assist with serving and delivery later this afternoon. Over by the bandstand, she could hear the high-school band practicing for their mini concert later in the day. The flea market and vendor area were bustling with activity as well. She knew that the handmade crafts, soaps, lotions, and jewelry would be sure to entice visitors.

Rita and Stephanie prepared a large container of lemonade using the fresh water hydrant conveniently located by their booth. Ken Jackson and the rest of the library board had also delivered a small freezer to store ice. The cookies were attractively displayed in a beautiful basket. The rest of the supplies for signing up for a library card and a pamphlet displaying the services offered at the library were also arranged perfectly on the counter area. Stephanie had also arranged a book display showing some of the books offered at the library and available for check out over the festival with the proof of a library card.

"Are you enjoying your position at the library?" inquired Rita.

"Oh, yes very much so. I have always enjoyed reading myself, and when I moved to this area, obtaining a library card was one of my first tasks. I also have my teaching certification, and once Mrs. Stevens returns to the library after her surgery, I plan to substitute teach this fall."

"That is a wonderful plan. Substitute teachers are a valuable resource to the school district. It will also be a step in to securing a permanent position should one open up. I taught for thirty-five years, and finally decided I was ready to retire. Teaching is a rewarding profession, but you also know when it is time for the younger generation to take your place."

Smiling in response, Stephanie watched a young mother navigate the crowds, pushing a stroller and securing a four- or five-year-old by the hand. She secretly longed for a child and quietly reminisced about the plans her and Jake had decided. They were going to start their family this summer. She was not going to cry, she told herself. God had new plans for her, she was positive, and she would continue to pray for peace.

At around 12:00 p.m., a lively bunch of teenagers approached the library booth and announced that Mr. Greyson, the school principal, had released them early to come and see what their volunteer duties consisted of. Stephanie was happy to show them the kid's activities and explain how to take tickets and reward winners. They were delighted to get started. They were also told they could have a lemonade and a cookie for assisting with the library fundraiser today.

By the beginning of the afternoon, the crowds had picked up. School children were happily exploring the petting zoo over on the far side of the festival grounds. Lemonade was selling consistently as the heat of the day demanded a refreshing drink. Parents approached the booth, and Stephanie introduced herself and had signed up five new library cardholders. A local organization that was just beginning also inquired about renting a space at the library for a minimal fee to hold their monthly meetings. Everyone that Stephanie met was friendly and receptive to learning about the library's offerings while their children engaged in the kid activities. Midafternoon, Ken Jackson came by and asked how things were going.

THE INHERITANCE

"Very well. We have signed up five new library cardholders, sold over fifty glasses of lemonade, and the kids are really enjoying the kid activities. I will need to stop by the library later and get some more bookmarks if tomorrow continues to be as busy as today," Stephanie remarked.

"I am always happy to hear more people interested in using the services of the library. I will stop by later this evening before you close to collect the change box and get it ready for a new day tomorrow. Keep up the excellent work, er, Stephanie," he assured her.

The volunteers changed at three, and Stephanie continued to answer questions from people who stopped by the booth. Trina and little Bobby came by in the stroller around four.

"Are you enjoying the first day of the festival?" asked Trina.

"Oh yes, we have been consistently busy selling tickets for the children's activities, selling lemonade and cookies, and signing people up for new cards."

Melanie, the volunteer from three to nine, suggested that Stephanie take a break and walk around with Trina for a bit.

"We will manage just fine. My daughter is coming by in a minute, and she can help me if it gets really busy. Go see what the festival is all about," encouraged Melanie.

"Okay, thanks. I won't be gone long, and should you need me, my number is on the paper inside the change box."

Stephanie and Trina headed toward all of the festival activities.

"My parents are coming by to collect Bobby in a little while so that I can work my shift at the chicken-and-noodle dinner. I am going to run a dinner out to John during my shift as that is my main job today—the delivery of orders," Trina informed her.

The two women headed for the vendor tent and walked slowly by looking at all the colorful and enticing display of goods for sale.

"There sure are a lot of people here today," remarked Stephanie.

"Oh, the crowds will pick up later this evening too. The music always draws a large crowd, and the chicken-and-noodle dinner takes advantage of all the crowds as well. Last year, we served over five hundred meals, I believe."

They continued through the long display of vendors and exited on the other end. Heading their way was Justin.

"Hi, Stephanie and Trina. My, I haven't seen you in a number of years."

"Hello, Justin," Trina answered enthusiastically. "I am so happy to see that you have returned to the area, and the opening of the vet clinic will be a boost to the town's economy as well. I didn't realize you had met Stephanie."

"Yes, we met up at the library one afternoon several weeks ago," answered Stephanie.

"I was summoned here to check on one of the sheep at the petting zoo," replied Justin. "So I should probably head on over and see what is going on there. I hope to see you both again soon."

As he left, Trina turned toward Stephanie with a tilt of her head and a questioning look on her face. "And why haven't you mentioned meeting Justin to me?"

"Well, I am at a crossroads as to how to handle meeting up with him. He came in to the library one day asking about a book in a series, and we realized who each other was by accident. When John heard the commercial on TV for the new vet clinic, he got very quiet, as if he wasn't sure how to react or what exactly to explain to me. I haven't told him either about meeting Justin. Jake always told me that the rift between Justin and his father was difficult to explain and it was best left alone for the time being. I always felt that Jake wanted to approach a reconciliation too. Justin wants to mend the rift and has asked me to initiate a meeting between him and his father. He feels that a go-between might soften the initial meeting. He also implored many times that he doesn't intend to create a bad relationship between John and me either. It is so confusing. And then last week when John had his episode and the doctor visits, I put off telling him, and now I guess I am unsure how to proceed," finished Stephanie.

Grabbing her friend by the arm, Trina indicated her support by saying, "I am sure you do have a lot of concerns about how to proceed. Just know that I am a good sounding board if you need to talk."

THE INHERITANCE

"Thanks, Trina. I do appreciate it. I was not trying to keep secrets. As I said, I just was trying to work it out in my head, and with all of the festival preparation, I kind of put it in the back of my mind for now."

"I understand, I really do." Trina side hugged her friend. Then she noticed her parents heading their way to collect little Bobby.

After making sure her parents had all of Bobby's things, Trina and Stephanie headed back. Trina was going to the church women's booth to begin her shift serving chicken and noodles; and Stephanie, after giving Trina her order for some chicken and noodles, headed back to the library booth.

"Another family signed up for a library card while you were away," Melanie conveyed enthusiastically as Stephanie entered through the side of the tent.

"That is wonderful! This is just the first day, and already we have signed up several for new library cards. I am happy to know that we are able to share all the library has to offer," Stephanie shared.

By six o'clock, crowds had really started attending the festival. A band was preparing for the evening's entertainment as indicated by the plucking of guitars and pounding of the drums to test for sound. You could feel the excitement and camaraderie in the air as people strode by most stopping for a refreshing glass of lemonade or allowing their children to obtain tickets for the games. Stephanie and her volunteers were kept busy with serving lemonade or answering questions about the library.

An older man approached the booth and inquired about Mrs. Stevens.

"Where is she this evening?" he wanted to know.

"Mrs. Stevens has had a knee replacement and is recovering at her daughter's house for the next several weeks. I am Stephanie Wilkes, the temporary librarian."

"Oh, I guess, I didn't realize Betty was having her knee replaced. Good for her as I know it was becoming increasingly harder for her to walk comfortably. My name is Peter Samuels, and we were neighbors before I moved to Casper to be closer to my son. We just had to come back for the festival. I haven't missed one in seventy years! It has

61

definitely grown over the years. Nice to see the library as a focal point for the community. It was nice meeting you, Stephanie, and good luck with the library," he said. Then he moved on down the walkway toward the larger tent set aside for listening to the music.

As the evening progressed, Stephanie enjoyed sitting back and watching the people as they strolled from one booth or activity to the next. Ken Jackson came by to collect the change box before Stephanie closed down for the evening. He said he would return again in the morning with more change. Zipping the tent closed, Stephanie turned upon hearing Justin's voice.

"May I walk you to your car?" he asked.

"Uh, well, sure," Stephanie stammered.

They headed toward the parking lot.

"I am sure you have had a long day."

"Yes, I was here at ten o'clock this morning and plan to be back again same time tomorrow."

"There sure are a lot of people at the festival this year. It has been a few years, of course, since I attended one. There are lots of new booths and a lot more activities for the kids," Justin remarked.

"Well, as I think I mentioned, this was my first day of ever attending. Jake and I were not married at this time last year. I was at home in Iowa with my parents, working a part-time job up until the wedding."

"So I have, uh, filled you in on the background of my family. But I guess I am being remorseful in not having asked about yours."

"I grew up in a large town just outside of Des Moines. My parents still live there. Mom is a teacher. She is preparing to retire in a few years. Dad worked in the business world and still does. My brothers—I have two—are still in college. They enjoy helping my uncle Wayne on his farm in the summers and on breaks. I have gained a little knowledge of small rural towns through them, I guess," Stephanie finished.

"So I am not trying to pry, but are you planning on staying in this area?" asked Justin.

Seeming to ponder that question, Stephanie finally answered, "I have grown to love this community. Trina and Brian have been amaz-

THE INHERITANCE

ing friends. They have helped me through Jake's unexpected death immensely. Your father and I have discussed our living arrangements. We have been an amazing support for each other. He asked me several months ago if I was happy here and would I consider staying. He really is a sweet man. Now I have this job, although only temporarily, that I have really enjoyed so far. My parents have of course encouraged me to return home to Iowa, but I have told them I don't want that either. Oftentimes, I feel like I really need to make a decision that will impact the rest of my life. I have my teaching degree, and I do want to teach one day. I am sorry it seems as if I am telling you more than you asked."

Listening intently, Justin reassured her, "No, I asked, and I really am interested."

Arriving at the car, Stephanie told Justin thanks for the conversation and that she hoped to see him again soon before backing out of her spot and heading home.

Justin stood there for a moment, contemplating Stephanie's words, before heading to his own truck for the drive back to his place.

15

The remaining two days of the town's festival passed rather quickly. Several families were signed up for library cards. The kids seemed to really enjoy returning often to play the games for a chance to win free books. The headliner for the festival, a rising country music star, was due to take the stage this evening at seven. Tomorrow would be the closing community church service. Stephanie and her list of volunteers were working on closing up the activities and lemonade servings.

As the festival was winding down, the committee volunteers would begin dismantling the booths and cleaning areas of the park. The petting zoo had already been taken down and the animals returned to their respective farms. Stephanie had seen Justin a few times and waved as he was called to attend to an animal but had not actually talked to him. She was hoping to talk John into coming into town for the community service tomorrow. Trina had been wonderful in making sure John had food from the women's church booth. She enjoyed her job of taking food to several shut-ins and call-in orders. She also stopped in to talk with Stephanie several times. They had managed to go and see more of the festival area and grab food to enjoy. Now a rolling cart was due to arrive at the stand in a few minutes to load up the supplies and take down the tent. Stephanie was pleased with the outcome of the booth and had met many new people from the area. She was also eager to plan some new programs to draw in the families that had signed up for the upcoming weeks.

"Stephanie," called Ken Jackson, hoping to gain her attention as he hurried toward the booth. "The library board and I are very

THE INHERITANCE

pleased with the booth's outcomes. I will be in to the library on Monday morning to go over things with you."

"Thank you, Mr. Jackson. Of course, that would be wonderful. I will plan to see you then."

Finishing packing up and loading the cart took very little time with the help of the volunteers. Susan's van was loaded and would be unloaded on Monday evening at the library with the help of even more volunteers.

Waving goodbye and thanking everyone for their successful event, Stephanie headed over to the bandstand. Trina and Brian would be waiting near the bandstand and saving a seat so they could all enjoy the evening's performance.

Finding Trina and Brian in the growing crowd was not hard. Trina was waving her over to the empty seat next to her. As she approached them, she noticed Justin sitting on the other side of Brian.

"Hello, everyone," Stephanie called out as she sat down.

"Hey, Stephanie. Justin tells me he has met you already, so I guess we don't need introductions," commented Brian.

With a nod of her head and a smile, Stephanie prepared herself to enjoy the country music and the soft breeze blowing on this sultry night.

"I bet you are ready for some downtime," Trina asked.

"Yes, this festival has been very nice, and I have met several families whom have signed up for library cards and plan to attend some of the upcoming events. Now I just need to get busy planning those events," Stephanie replied with a chuckle.

The band members came up onstage and were warming up their instruments when the mayor came forward to the microphone.

"Welcome, citizens of Braintenburg. We have had another excellent festival, and I would personally like to thank all of the vendors and committees who have done an excellent job on this year's event. Tonight, we are wrapping up our delightful festival with the grand performance of John Ingles. Please put your hands together to welcome John to our great town, and I hope you all enjoy the show!"

MARIE MALONE

The main event began, and for the next hour, they all sat back and enjoyed the country music. Midway through, the band decided to take a short fifteen-minute break. Brian offered to go get some cool drinks for the group, and Justin went with him.

"So what is going on with the Justin and John reunion?" inquired Trina.

"I haven't had a moment to pursue that further. You could have warned me about him being here this evening."

"Justin and Brian grew up together, and they were and are still great friends. It is interesting to see that they can just take up where they left off. Justin explained to us earlier about the last four years of his life. Brian is excited to have his old friend back and eager to use the services of the new veterinary offices too. I anticipate us spending a lot of time together again. I hope it won't be awkward for you either," finished Trina.

"I hope not either. I've decided that tomorrow afternoon I am going to mention all of this to John, and hopefully, we can find some time to reconcile things. At least, that is my hope and prayer. I often get the feeling that John wants a chance to see his son again. I know from having spoken to Justin that is his deep desire as well. So we will continue to pray that this will all work out soon."

The men returned with drinks, and Justin handed one to Stephanie with a smile. She murmured her thanks as the concert prepared to go on.

Later, as the four were returning to the parking lot, it so happened that Brian and Trina were walking a bit ahead, holding hands; so Justin and Stephanie fell into step together.

"Justin, I just wanted you to know that I have plans to speak to John tomorrow afternoon about our meeting."

"Okay. I, of course, am interested in hearing how that goes. Do you mind if I give you my number, and if it works, ask you to give me a call tomorrow evening? I am sorry it is just that I am anxious to approach my dad and see if we can make amends."

"I do understand, and I want that for the both of you as well."

Justin handed Stephanie a business card with the number for the clinic and his personal number listed on it.

THE INHERITANCE

"Okay then, I will talk to you soon," Stephanie said.

On the drive home, Stephanie replayed the last few days in her mind, especially all the parts involving Justin and her part in this reconciliation. She needed to have a plan on how to approach John. She had never had a problem discussing things with him, and she prayed that this time wouldn't be any different.

16

Sunday morning there was a beautiful sunrise almost an answer to a prayer. Stephanie felt an overwhelming feeling of comfort as she prepared a picnic basket for after the morning service in the park. She was aware of John's reluctance to attend the outdoor service, but this day was a new beginning, and she was going to take advantage of it.

"Are you about ready, John?" Stephanie inquired. "It is such a beautiful morning, and I am so filled with joy in this day." She wasn't giving him a chance to say he wasn't going, so she implied that she expected him to accompany her.

John entered the kitchen with a hesitant look on his face. Stephanie quickly linked arms with him and headed toward the back door.

"I am not sure I am up for going to services in the park. Everyone will ask why I didn't attend any of the other festival activities."

"John, you have never missed a church service since I have known you, and today is no exception. You do not have to explain to anyone why you were not around these past few days. Everyone will be happy to see you today as always. Now let's go. We don't want to be late for the opening songs."

They walked down the porch steps, and Stephanie placed the picnic basket in the back seat. John sat in the passenger seat, still appearing a bit hesitant to go.

Stephanie chatted about the library booth and its success all the way to the city park. When they got there, Stephanie quickly found a parking spot, and they walked toward the gathering crowds.

THE INHERITANCE

"Good morning, John...Stephanie. Nice to see you both on this glorious morning," greeted Pastor Steve.

"Yes, it is a beautiful day. I am looking forward to this change of having an outdoor service. I have never attended one before."

Stephanie eagerly continued on toward the rows of chairs set up for the service. Suddenly, she remembered that she had mentioned to Justin about attending the service in the park. How would she handle a confrontation between John and Justin here in view of the town? Would it be awkward if they didn't even acknowledge each other or worse start an argument? She quickly scanned the crowd but did not spot Justin anywhere. Then, just as quickly as her fears and anxiety arose, a peace came over her. She knew that it would be just fine.

The service music began with an upbeat song, and just the combined voices raising praises to heaven brought tears of happiness. The guest speaker brought a message of community and how working together to spread God's word was a sign of devotion.

After the service ended, families gathered at tables to share food and talk. John was involved in a conversation with some local ranchers and appeared to be having a wonderful time. She met up with Trina, Brian, and little Bobby. They planned to sit together and share in the warm day with great food.

Once lunch was finished, people started to pick up chairs and wipe down tables. The park committee would get everything stored, and the park would be returned to normal in quick order.

Waving goodbye to Trina, Stephanie and John walked quietly toward the car.

"I am glad you talked me into attending the service today. The message was great, and seeing some old friends definitely boosted my spirits. So thanks, Stephanie."

"I am glad you enjoyed the day. I was hoping once we get home you and I could sit on the porch and talk a bit. Would that be okay with you?"

"Sure, Stephanie. I am always willing to listen and discuss things."

The drive home was quick, and once the picnic basket was emptied of the containers of food, Stephanie poured them each a glass of lemonade, and they sat in the rocking chairs. Stephanie was working through in her mind how to broach the subject of Justin and sent up a quick prayer that God would be with her in her words.

"John, I hope that we can have a good talk now. I want you to know that you mean the world to me, and I treasure our relationship and everything you have provided for me."

"Stephanie," John interrupted, "you are scaring me. You are not thinking of leaving this ranch, are you?"

"Oh no, Dad. I am sorry, I didn't mean to give you worries. I enjoy this community so much. I really enjoy my part-time job, and while I do not know what the future holds for me right now, I am so happy to be here."

"Oh, okay. That is a huge relief," John exclaimed.

"I guess I just don't know how to tell you what I need to say. So here it is. I met Justin for the first time a few days ago at the library. He came in to borrow a book from a series he was reading and was just as surprised to meet me as I was him." She let that sink in for a moment before continuing. "We met the next day again, and he explained your discord to me."

John rose up from the chair and walked over to the edge of the porch and leaned on the railing. Head bowed, he sighed and appeared to be struggling with the news.

"Dad, are you okay?" At his brief nod, she continued, "I just want you to know that Justin is very eager to reconcile with you. He regrets the time that has passed, and he wants to resolve your differences. Do you feel that that is something you would be interested in as well? I have noticed you examining the flyer in the mail, and I somehow feel that now is a great time to work on that. What do you say?"

"Stephanie, let me explain, if you will. When Justin chose to leave the farm and pursue his veterinary degree, a part of me didn't understand how he could choose a different path than what we had discussed, the three of us, his whole life. I know that I am a stubborn man, and I lost my temper that day and said things I regret. I had just lost my precious Margorie, and now I was also losing my son. I was so angry with him and God as well for taking my sweet Margorie way

THE INHERITANCE

too early. Jake tried to explain Justin's thinking to me, but I didn't want to hear it. I asked him to let him go as well and that we would not have anything to do with him. Now I also know that was wrong asking Jake to carry that burden. He and Justin got along so well as brothers, and I know my ultimatum forced him to choose. I will live with that for the rest of my life. Last week when Pastor Steve had his sermon on forgiveness, it gave me cause to stop and think. I want to move forward as well. I feel God has given me this opportunity with Justin returning to the area and opening his vet practice. These are definite signs that we need to work on our relationship and see if there is a chance we can become father and son again."

"Oh, Dad, that makes my heart happy. How about we invite Justin over for dinner one night this week?"

"Yes, that would be good. I assume you know how to get in touch with him?"

"Yes, I met up with him at the closing concert last night, and he asked that I call him after discussing things with you. I will do that and see what evening works the best for him, okay?"

"Sure, Stephanie, that sounds like a fine idea. Now I think I will go watch a little TV and relax in my recliner."

"Sure, Dad." Stephanie watched as John walked into the house and noticed a slightly less hump to his posture as if a weight had been lifted. She certainly hoped this would go well. She pulled the business card from her jeans pocket and dialed Justin's number.

He answered on the first ring as if he was waiting to hear from her.

"Stephanie?" he answered excitedly.

"Yes, good afternoon, Justin. I just wanted to call and let you know that I have talked with John about your reconciliation, and he was absolutely for it. He seems to have a load of regret for how things went with the two of you. So I am asking would you be willing to come for dinner one evening this next week, and perhaps we can move forward with a new relationship for the two of you?"

"I would love to do that."

"Well, how about Tuesday evening then? I get home from the library around two, and if you would plan to arrive at five, we could start with dinner and see how that goes."

"I will be there. And, Stephanie, I don't know how to begin to thank you for being the go-between. I sincerely appreciate it, and I just want you to know that I look forward to getting to know you."

"Okay then, we will see you Tuesday evening," Stephanie finished hurriedly.

A huge part of her mind was devoted to this new beginning for John and Justin. Another part of her mind was thinking about the friendship she had started with Justin. She was not ready to admit that feelings of more than friendship could be there. Her heart was still healing over the loss of Jake. Their one-year anniversary would have been in a couple of weeks, and she wasn't sure how she was going to prepare for that.

Later in the evening, as she was preparing a light supper, she told John about the dinner plans; and he appeared to be ready as well.

17

The next day, shortly after Stephanie opened for the day, Ken Jackson entered the library with Susan Phillips alongside him.

"Good morning, Stephanie," he greeted her.

She noticed he didn't have to be corrected to call her Stephanie instead of Mrs. Wilkes.

"Hello, it is a beautiful day outside this morning," Stephanie returned the greeting.

"We are here to go over the festival's report with you. Let me begin by saying how appreciative the library board is with your willingness to organize the booth and events on such short notice. Mrs. Stevens is a great librarian, but your youthfulness and agility"—he grinned—"are what has made this event possible.

"We signed up twenty-five new families for library cards this past week. That is a big difference and will make using the library exactly what was the desire of the library board. Of course, fourteen of those families will pay for the services as they are outside the city limits and therefore not able to utilize city taxes, which pay for the library. That alone generated over $300. Then with the lemonade sales and purchases of the raffle tickets, we brought in almost $5,000 for the library. That is way more than our original expectations, and we couldn't be more excited with the opportunities this revenue will provide."

"Well, thank you for your information. I sincerely enjoyed planning for the event, and I am thrilled to hear about the money generated," Stephanie returned with a smile.

"We would like to hear some of your thoughts on what the library could use the money for. A volunteer mentioned that you were sharing some thoughts the other day," Susan asked.

"Yes!" Stephanie returned excitedly. "I hope to start a reading program that will encourage the children to read a certain number of books and earn a reward card that would be punched for each book read. Then they could redeem their reward cards for free ice cream or other small prizes. I would like to host an author to read to children, and even an author for adults. We could also offer a book club for children and adults alike with a featured book of the month. I was hoping to liven up the children's area with pillows and a new coat of paint and some benches for Story Hour." Then she seemed to stop suddenly. "I am sorry, I mean I don't want to infringe on what Mrs. Stevens would also like as she will be the one to implement these changes when she returns."

"Well, that brings us to our next reason for meeting with you today," Ken added. "I received a phone call from Mrs. Stevens herself yesterday. Her surgery went well and recovery is going well too. She is enjoying the time spent with her children and grandchildren. She would like to retire from her position here in the library as she plans to stay on with her daughter. So we are here to offer you the full-time position of head librarian for the library. Are you interested?"

A shocked look came over Stephanie's face for a moment. She was not expecting this.

"I...yes, I would love to be the librarian," Stephanie answered excitedly.

"Great, then we will discuss your salary at the next board meeting, which will be next week. We can go over your hours and additional staff you might want to employ for assistance with the programs. If you could please think on those ideas and get us a list of programs and potential costs that we could also discuss at the board meeting, that would be extremely helpful," finished Ken.

"We will let you get on with your day then and look forward to talking more with you soon. Thank you again, Stephanie."

They both turned to leave the library, and Stephanie seemed to fall into her chair in shock.

THE INHERITANCE

She was going to be the full-time librarian! It was like a dream. All of her ideas could possibly take place. Reaching absently for the phone, she dialed Trina's number.

"Hello," Trina answered in an anxious voice.

"Hi, friend, it's Stephanie. You sound like you are out of breath."

"Just chasing a toddler and trying to load the washer at the same time. What's up with you?"

"I just got the best news, and I had to call. I was just offered the full-time head librarian position," she said excitedly. "Mrs. Stevens has decided to retire."

"Wow, that is wonderful. I am really happy for you, Stephanie. I know you have some exciting ideas planned."

A loud crash could be heard in the background.

"Oh no, I am so sorry, Steph, I have to go." Trina hung up the phone.

Stephanie smiled as she hung up. She knew that Trina had her hands full with little Bobby. She knew that she would have a chance to talk with Trina later when little Bobby went down for an afternoon nap. She would need to fill her in on the upcoming reunion between John and Justin.

The day progressed with several of the new sign-ups coming in to the library to check out the offerings. She especially enjoyed showing the children's section to young parents and explaining that it would be updated very soon. In between assisting patrons with book check outs and answering questions, Stephanie worked on her proposal for the library board meeting. She wanted her proposal to be both eye-catching and informative. Designing a layout and tweaking it would be done over the next few days. She also needed to think about how to utilize an assistant librarian. She knew that a few volunteers would be interested in a paid position if even for a limited number of hours a week. She hoped to keep her hours and include some time off to pursue getting more involved in the community.

Around three, the library phone rang, and Stephanie answered.

"Hello, this is Stephanie, head librarian. How can I assist you?"

"Trying out your new title, are you?" Trina chuckled.

"Oh, hi, Trina. Yes, I just wanted to hear it with my own ears, I guess," Stephanie answered on a chuckle.

"Well, it sounds very you, my friend. Again, congratulations, and I am so very pleased to hear this. It means you will be staying around. I am sorry I had to hang up on you this morning. Bobby is learning to pull on cords, and he found the lamp in the living room. Luckily, it didn't break, but it scared him, so I can only hope he is learning not to do it again. You must have gotten a good report from the festival?"

"Yes, Ken and Susan were in this morning. We signed up twenty-five new families for library cards! The children's games and raffle also did remarkably. The board is very pleased. Ken said that Mrs. Stevens called him yesterday and said that she wanted to continue staying with her daughter's family even after recovery and was turning in her resignation. I really had no idea she was even considering retirement when she left here a month ago. Oh, I also have some other exciting news to share. Yesterday, John and I had a discussion about reuniting with Justin, and he agreed that it was time to meet and talk things over, so I am having Justin over for dinner tomorrow night. Any suggestions on meal ideas?"

"Wow, you have had a very busy last few days!" Trina offered. "I haven't gotten the whole story from you yet about meeting Justin for the first time."

"I know, and I hope we can have lunch soon and get caught up."

"As far as dinner, you can't go wrong with your fried chicken."

"I was thinking that as well. Thanks for the confirmation."

"Well, let me know how it goes tomorrow night, won't you?"

"Yes! I most definitely will. Now I am going to have to hang up as another family just walked in. I will talk to you soon." Stephanie hung up the phone and greeted the new family, preparing to answer any questions and showing them the arrangement of the library.

* * * * *

It had been a great day at the library. Stephanie felt like she had accomplished a lot. She introduced two new families to the workings

THE INHERITANCE

of the library, helped several patrons locate books to their interest, had time to work on her proposals for the upgrades to the library, and silently celebrate her new position as head librarian.

On her way home later that evening, Stephanie smiled to herself in anticipation of sharing her news with John. It would have been an exciting moment to share with Jake as well. They would have celebrated. He would have been happy for her giving her kisses and hugs. That is what she missed the most, the shared camaraderie and affection. Would she find that again with someone new? She reflected for a moment. Jake and her had met at college at a social gathering for members of the Christian sorority and fraternities that they had both been in. They seemed to connect on several levels. They only had two months before he graduated and moved back home. He had managed to come visit her on a few weekends, and she made the trip to the farm one weekend to be introduced to his dad. It was that trip when Jake surprised her and asked her to marry him. She was so happy that she quickly agreed. She still had a year of college to finish at the time, and wedding plans were a part of that year. Jake had told her to do whatever she wanted but requested that they get married in the backyard of his home. It had been where John and Margorie had married thirty years prior. Since it seemed to be the one thing Jake desired, she agreed. Her family supported their decision. Stephanie only had made the one trip to the family farm but found the peacefulness and canopy of trees to be a beautiful spot for an outdoor wedding, something she had desired as well. She had always worked in a local children's shelter for each summer and on breaks when attending college, so she had not had the opportunity to become so familiar with the town. One quick trip to the farm several weeks before the wedding to organize the setup and food delivery was her only time to familiarize herself. After a brief weekend honeymoon, she and Jake had moved into the family home with John. He had asked that they do so while she and Jake planned the building of their new home the following spring. That is all they had had time for, some brief plans, before Jake's untimely death.

Arriving at the house, Stephanie noticed John out in the pasture herding some cattle, so she went on into the house to begin dinner preparations. A part of her filed away the sad memories of Jake's passing. Another part was excited for the new opportunities this job would provide. She missed Jake, but she also knew that God had plans for her.

At dinner, Stephanie relayed her wonderful news to John, and he was delighted for her. They discussed their dinner plans for the following night and inviting Justin back into the family. John appeared nervous for the meeting, so she asked him what concerned him the most.

"Oh, Stephanie, I am not sure. I want this reconciliation to happen, but I know there is a lot of pain involved as well. Will we be able to mend that?" he asked.

"John, I think in talking with Justin that he will be as anxious and eager as you are. You are father and son, and that bond can't be broken so much that it can't be mended."

"Thank you for that comforting thought."

After dinner had been cleared up, Stephanie went to sit on the porch and enjoy the setting sun and soft breeze. Earlier, when she had thoughts of Jake and a promise so quickly ended, she also wanted to think for a minute on her growing friendship with Justin. She thought back to the day when he had walked into the library, God's answer to a prayer, and the momentary pause when their eyes met. He had been surprised and totally didn't expect to meet her that day. She had been wondering as well how she would initiate a meeting between John and Justin, and God had the answer. Justin was certainly an attractive man. She sensed an attraction between them the evening that he had walked her to her car at the festival. He had listened to her, really listened, and she now realized how special that had made her feel. Would it be awkward to start a relationship with Justin? What would others think? Should she be even having these thoughts? So many questions in her head, and no immediate answers available. She finally decided to head into the house for bed and pray that God would steer her thoughts and actions in the right direction.

18

Tuesdays were a short day for Stephanie. She opened the library at ten and worked on finishing her proposal for the library board. At two, her volunteer, Beth, would take over for the rest of the afternoon until the library closed at five. When Beth arrived, she asked her to sit for a moment to discuss something.

"Beth, I have been offered the position of head librarian. It is not official until the library board meeting next week."

"Oh, I am excited for you, Stephanie," Beth declared.

"Thank you, but what I also wanted to ask you is if you would be interested in being recommended for the part-time associate librarian. It is a paid position. I know you have volunteered here for some time with Mrs. Stevens, and I feel you are familiar with the library already. How do you feel? Would that be something I could ask the board for?"

"Oh, I...well, yes, I think so. When Mrs. Stevens asked me to volunteer a few hours a week, it provided me an opportunity to add to my resume. She couldn't offer me a job, so being the avid reader I am, I looked at this as an opportunity to check new releases and get books to read. I am looking for some part-time work to supplement my other jobs on the weekends. And since the library is not open on the weekends, I think I could work that out. So, yes! Stephanie, I am interested, and thank you for considering me."

"My proposal would be for about twenty to twenty-five hours a week. I have plans to offer some classes and contests for children. I want to invite guest speakers to the library for adults and maybe even open the library to some evening hours. We could alternate the evening times."

"I work at the restaurant across town on the weekends as a waitress. I have to rely on tips to make a decent wage. With this added opportunity, I could find my own place eventually. Oh, I do watch a neighbor's children when she needs to run errands, but she does that on mornings and not every day, so we could work on our schedule. I would have to ask her to pick her days for errands."

"Okay then, I will add that information to my proposal. Thank you. Now I need to head on over to the store before going home. I have dinner plans for later, so I need to pick up a few items. I will see you again on Thursday."

"Yes, I will be here, and thank you again, Stephanie. I am excited to work alongside you."

Stephanie quickly went out to her car and drove to the local grocery. She needed a few things for the upcoming dinner this evening.

* * * * *

Dinner preparations were almost finished. The table was set. John had come in about an hour ago and decided he needed a shower to wash off the sweat of the day. She looked at the clock, 4:40. She was certain that Justin would be right on time. John came into the kitchen.

"Something smells delicious in here," he commented.

"Thanks. It is fried chicken and potatoes with salad and rolls. Plus I made your favorite dessert, butter pecan cake with cream cheese icing."

"Oh my, that sounds delicious. I am sure that things will go over well tonight, Stephanie. I promise that I will make every effort to see that it happens."

"Dad, I know how much you want this, and I feel it will be a good evening as well."

A few minutes later they heard a truck pull into the driveway. John went out onto the porch. He stood there until Justin turned his truck off and opened the door to exit.

THE INHERITANCE

After a few seconds of just staring at each other, John said, "Good evening, Justin. Glad you could make it to have dinner with us."

"Hello, Dad. Thanks for inviting me."

Justin started for the porch steps as John started down the steps. They met at the base of the steps and shook hands. John placed his other hand on Justin's extended arm and smiled.

"Son, I am very glad we have this opportunity to clear up our issues. I want to start by saying that I have wanted this to happen for some time, and I just didn't know how to begin."

"I have as well, Dad. Moving back here to my hometown has made that very clear to me."

"Well, let's go in and sit down for some dinner then, shall we?"

"Yes, that sounds wonderful. I haven't had a home cooked meal in quite some time. Everything looks wonderful here on the farm too, Dad. I noticed when I pulled in that you have new fencing and the barn has been painted. It always has been so peaceful here, and I have sincerely missed it and you."

Entering the kitchen, John smiled at Stephanie.

"I guess you two know each other. Why don't you go ahead and have a seat, Justin. Stephanie is an excellent cook, and I know she is almost ready to serve the food."

"Hello, Justin. Glad you could make it this evening." She glanced at the clock. Right on time as she had thought he might be.

"Hi, Stephanie. It sure smells delicious in here. I appreciate all of your work in preparing this evening's meal."

"What would you like to drink, Justin?" she asked "We have tea or lemonade."

"Tea is fine. Thank you, but I can help if you need me to."

"Oh no, I have it all ready to serve."

An offer to help with dinner? *What a gentleman*, she thought. John usually assisted with clearing the table most evenings but otherwise waited for her to set things out.

After plating the chicken and setting all the food on the table, Stephanie took her seat, and John reached for her hand and Justin's to say grace.

"Dear Lord, we thank you greatly for this opportunity to share a meal and a chance to come together to work on our differences. We ask your blessings on this food and this evening. In your name we pray, *Amen*."

"*Amen*," Stephanie and Justin echoed in return.

After everyone had food on their plate and had started eating, John spoke up.

"So, Justin, I know it has been a while since we were together. And I just want to say that I am so glad you are here this evening. I know that we have a lot of ground to cover, but I was hoping you could talk a little about your new business."

"Thanks, Dad. I am grateful to be here. Stephanie, everything is delicious!"

"Thanks."

"The new vet clinic will be opening in two weeks. I have gone into business with two colleagues of mine. We met in vet school and finished our residencies within fifty miles of each other. Mike's uncle is Doc Stevens, and when he announced his retirement to take effect at the end of this month, Mike approached him about buying his business. I know Doc Stevens has worked long and hard to establish his customers, so we felt we would have a good solid business here. Craig is the biggest investor at the moment. His dad owns a chain of hardware stores and other businesses. We decided a new facility that would serve not only large animals but small pets as well. Along with that, we wanted to have a facility that could perform surgeries on animals if needed. That is my skill, I suppose."

John's eyebrows rose. "You are a surgeon?" He sounded impressed.

"Well, yes, I completed my residency last spring and can perform surgery on small and large animals alike. It is what I am truly interested in. Mike wants to be the traveling vet and go on calls to farms. I suppose we will all do some of that as well. Craig wants to tend to dogs and cats mostly but has skills in tending to large animals as well. We all seem to fit together and get along great. I came here in June to see to the completion of the facility while Craig and Mike finished working on the farms they have been on through the

THE INHERITANCE

summer. They will be arriving next week, and we are going to spend a week furnishing the place and getting ready for the open house. I sincerely hope you both plan on attending?"

"Sure, we would like that chance. I have used Doc Stevens as our vet for a number of years as you probably remember. He told me that his business would be in great hands when he announced his retirement last December, but he didn't go into details at that time. I saw the flyer in the mail a couple weeks back, and that is when I noticed your picture and when I started hoping we could work on our own relationship."

"It is what I sincerely want as well, Dad," Justin remarked.

Stephanie had sat quietly listening to Justin tell his story, and now that dinner was coming to a close, she offered John and Justin a chance to go sit out on the porch while she cleaned up and brought the dessert out.

"Oh no, I am going to help you with the cleanup. You've already done all the hard work here. This meal was delicious, I will say again. The chicken was exceptional, your biscuits so moist and tasty. I haven't enjoyed a meal like this in quite some time."

After attempting again to tell him she could manage and he insisting on helping, they finished the task of putting away leftovers and loading the dishwasher.

"Now please both of you go on out to the porch and relax. I will bring dessert and join you momentarily."

John and Justin walked out to the porch. She wanted to give them a few minutes to talk between themselves before she joined them anyway.

John began after sitting down. "Son, I know that I have been a stubborn man, and I hope you will accept my apologies for things I said to you so long ago."

Justin raised his hand slightly. "Dad, I need to apologize as well. I just knew years ago that running the farm and all that you do here was not what would have made me happy. I know this farm means the world to you. I do appreciate that, and I understand it. I needed to find my place in this world, and working with animals is what makes me happiest. I am most sorry for staying away as long as I have. I guess it was my pride that wanted to finish my degree and prove that I could make you proud. I managed to stay in touch with Jake for about six months after, but then I felt it wasn't fair for him to be torn between the two of us, so I lost touch with him as well," he finished sadly.

"That is on me as well, I am afraid. I asked him not to keep you informed and that if you were truly interested in changing things, it would have to be you that made the first move. I encouraged him to let you go. Now I live with those regrets. I lost both of my sons, and I just didn't know how to go on for some time there six months ago. Stephanie has been such a blessing to me. She has agreed to stay here, and together we have worked through our grief. They were barely married four months when the accident happened. I know they had plans to build their own place and start a family in the future, but that came to a sad end. This job at the library has definitely given her some joy back in her life, and now I have an opportunity to work things out with you, so I feel God has blessed me through all this tragedy."

"Yes, I truly wish to work on building a better relationship with you too, Dad."

"How about our first step be you filling me in on what you did in vet school and from there on?" suggested John.

"I think I was more determined than ever after our disagreement, so when I returned to college, I only had a semester to go to finish my general studies. It helped a lot that my concentration was on science classes. I spoke to my counselor, and he said that two to three years with practicum would get my vet degree, so that is what I decided to do. I appreciate that you helped with my general studies degree, but I needed to find a way to pay for my continuing education, so I took a lot of odd jobs on weekends and breaks. One job, working for a farmer helped me deal a lot with my anger and stubbornness, I guess. Tim and his family invited me to church with them, and I met Pastor Rich. He offered some personal counseling, and there was a men's Bible study group that I joined. When classes finished, I needed a practicum site, so I accepted a position on a dairy farm in California. I still keep in touch with Pastor Rich and

THE INHERITANCE

some of the men from the group. My buddies from vet school, Mike and Steve, ironically accepted positions for their practicum in nearby towns. So we developed a bond, and that is how we came to think about the vet clinic here in town."

John sat, listening quietly to Justin tell his story, and was genuinely interested in all the details. He asked questions, and Justin answered with delight. He realized that this time was detrimental to starting a new beginning.

Stephanie came out with dessert, and the three of them sat quietly enjoying the evening sunset. When it was time to call it a night, Justin thanked Stephanie again for the delicious meal and, turning to his father, reached for his hand to shake it when John pulled him in for a hug.

"Justin, I am glad you joined us for this evening. I hope that we can continue to visit again soon. There is much more that I would like to hear about California and your future plans."

"Yes, sure, I'd like that as well. Next week, as I mentioned earlier, Mike and Steve are arriving. And we will need to devote a lot of time to the clinic. I've rented a large four-bedroom house, and we are thinking for the time being that we will manage to live together until we make further plans."

"Well, I know it is early, but I'd certainly like to meet them both sometime."

"The opening of the clinic is planned for the week after next, so I sincerely hope to see you both at the grand opening." Justin smiled and nodded as he inched his way toward the steps and his truck. "Good night." He waved and got in his truck and drove back toward town.

John turned toward Stephanie with the beginnings of tears in his eyes.

"Stephanie, I just want to express my appreciation once again for the part you've played in making this happen. I feel more relieved that I ever imagined and filled with some new hope."

"Dad, I am glad it is all working out. I want this for the both of you. I am enjoying getting to know Justin and look forward to more times together."

"I am going to bed now," John declared.

"Okay, Dad, I will see you in the morning. Good night."

Stephanie continued to sit on the porch watching the final descent of the sun and listening to the crickets and motions of the animals in the pasture. She felt relieved as well and sent up a prayer of thanksgiving that it had all worked out this evening and the future seemed promising. She realized that the anniversary of her and Jake's wedding would be in two weeks and reflected on how her life had changed in the past year. She missed Jake but was recognizing that she was also healing from the loss. A thought came to mind about starting a new relationship. She certainly wouldn't rush into anything, but she felt that staying here in Braintenburg was the right decision for her. A picture of Justin formed in her mind, and she was momentarily shocked. Their friendship was nice, and she wanted to continue that. They had had some nice discussions. *But a new relationship with her brother-in-law, was that the right thing?* she wondered. The chill of the night air sent her in to the house, and as she prepared for bed, she again asked God for guidance in her life and the decisions she had to make.

19

The next morning at the library, Stephanie continued to work on her plans for the library. She worked on a PowerPoint presentation for the library board meeting next week. Today was Children's Story Hour at three, so she also worked on preparing the story and snacks. Beth would be in at two to help with Story Hour and the craft they had planned. She was deep in thinking when her phone rang loudly. She had forgotten to turn the volume down, and that was even one of the rules for the library: phones on silent.

She quickly answered so as to silence the ringing.

"Hello, this is Stephanie, head librarian. How can I help you?"

"Oh, so now you are answering your personal phone this way too, huh." Trina chuckled.

"Oh gosh, Trina, I am so sorry, my mind was elsewhere. And I even forgot what phone I was answering. I didn't even look at caller ID."

"No worries," she answered on a laugh. "I was just wondering how last night's dinner arrangement went. I am anxious to hear."

"Yes. It really couldn't have gone any better. John was nervous when Justin pulled in the drive. Right on time, I might also mention. Dinner turned out great. I am glad you suggested the chicken. They were both very receptive to each other. At first, it was a lot of small talk through dinner. Then Justin helped me put away the leftovers and load the dishwasher before he and John went out to sit on the porch and talk. I left them out there to themselves for a while, but I heard voices, and when I went out for dessert, they were deep in conversation about Justin's life since college. And, Trina, when Justin prepared to leave, John reached out to hug him. It was an answer to a prayer."

"Well, that is fantastic news! Brian was hoping it was all working out for them as well. He mentioned at breakfast that he was so happy that his friend was back and he wanted to invite him out for a barbeque soon. I would expect you and John to attend as well."

"Thank you. That sounds like a wonderful time."

"Stephanie, are you okay as well? You mentioned that you were zoning out this morning. Everything okay with you?"

"Oh yes, Trina, I was working on progress plans for the board proposal next week and also thinking about Story Hour when you called. But there is something I'd like to talk over with you sometime as well."

"Sure, friend. My ears are always here." She chuckled.

"Okay well, I need to get back to my thinking, but maybe Saturday, we could talk some?"

"Absolutely! I will plan on that. Now I will let you go. But first, are you planning on attending movie night in the park on Friday?"

"Umm, yes, maybe. I will let you know."

"Okay, bye now."

Trina was such a great friend. She was so happy to have been introduced to her and Brian last summer before the wedding, and their friendship continued to blossom. Going to the movie night would be fun. The park held them every other Friday night in the summer months. It drew a large crowd, but going alone wasn't something she enjoyed either, and John was never one for going before. She knew that Brian and Trina would welcome her with them, but it was a chance at a date night for them as well. They got a sitter for little Bobby and planned a picnic and movie as a date night. She wouldn't want to impede on that. She was deep in thought on that when the front doors opened, and in walked Justin.

"Stephanie?" Justin called out when he realized she hadn't acknowledged him.

"Oh, good morning, Justin." She shook her head to clear her thoughts. "A bit of overthinking on my part. I am sorry."

Their eyes met, and a zing went through Stephanie's mind.

THE INHERITANCE

"No, that is fine. I just wanted to return this book and check out the next one in the series if I could"

Embarrassed and attempting to appear more with it, Stephanie quickly turned to her computer to check if the desired book was on the shelf. She tapped in the title, and it showed that it was available.

"Yes, it is on the shelf. Row ten, shelf three."

"Yes, I remember where I got this one." He grinned and started toward the section.

Oh, my word, Stephanie thought. *Get it together now. You are acting like a doofus. What is the matter with me today?*

Justin returned with the book in hand.

"I want to thank you once again for a great evening last night. I couldn't be more pleased with the way things are heading for Dad and I."

"Yes, John mentioned that as well."

"Good, good. I, uh, just finished this book last night after I returned home and thought I should, uh, come get the next one so I would have something to read this evening before bed," Justin finished.

"Right. Got to have a book to read." Stephanie smiled knowingly as she stamped in the due date.

Justin turned to leave and then turned back around and nervously asked, "Are you available for lunch tomorrow?"

"Uh, yes, I can be. It would have to be at one o'clock though. Thursdays are my early-out day, and Beth comes in as a volunteer. So I would have to wait for her to get here, and then I could join you."

"Good, I will be by at one o'clock then. Thanks."

Oh wow, what just happened? Stephanie asked herself. Did she just agree to a date with Justin? Maybe it wasn't a date, date. Maybe he just wanted to discuss something with her. She needed to get her head back into the business at hand and think more on this later.

The rest of the morning passed quickly, and by the time Beth arrived, Stephanie was back in librarian mode.

"Hi, Beth. Glad you are here. Story Hour keeps growing each week, and I anticipate a large crowd today."

89

"Oh, I am happy to assist where and when I can. I should also mention that since you said about this becoming a possible paid position, I am more excited than ever."

"Well, I sincerely believe that it will all happen. We just have to continue to pray and wait for the meeting next week."

Story Hour started at three, and six more children joined the group than had been there last week. Stephanie would have to make this note on her presentation as well. The children enjoyed the story and laughed often. They were all well behaved and polite when the snacks were shared. The art project took both sets of adult hands and another mother's hands but turned out perfectly. Story Hour usually turned into Story Hours by the time children checked out other books and clean up occurred. At five thirty, Stephanie locked the library doors and headed home.

On her drive home, her mind returned to the unexpected lunch invite for tomorrow. Again, she asked herself was it right to pursue another relationship so soon. Then she stopped and corrected herself maybe in her anxiousness to not be alone she was making more out of the lunch invite than what was there. She would just have to play it cool and wait and see.

John and Stephanie enjoyed dinner and talked about the farm events that were going on. John mentioned that in another few weeks' school would start again, and he would lose his summer help.

"Maybe, you need to consider hiring a full-time manager and helper, Dad."

"You know you are probably right. I have managed this farm with the occasional weekend help. Jake and I together had our hands full, and now that he is gone, I do need to think about hiring someone."

For a few moments, silence settled at the table. Then John spoke up.

"Stephanie, I really do not know what I would have done had you decided to return to your hometown. Having you here has made all the difference, and I don't think I have told you that enough."

THE INHERITANCE

"Oh, Dad, I know how hard it has been for the both of us. But Braintenburg has become my home now, and I am happy to be here with you."

"Well, I also know that you need to go on with your life as well. You are a young, attractive woman, and I want you to feel free to pursue other relationships. I know that Jake would have wanted you to be happy and fulfilled as well."

Stephanie once again thought about the upcoming lunch invite and promised herself once again not to put more hope into it than was called for.

"Well, let's not worry about any of that for now. You and Justin are working on developing a new beginning, and my job is exciting with the new possibilities as well."

They finished their meal and spent the rest of the evening watching a few shows on television.

20

The next morning Stephanie told John that she would be home a little earlier than normal but that she still had some things to take care of in town before coming home. She left for the library. She had wanted to talk with Trina but told herself that Saturday would be their girls' talk.

The morning passed quickly, and the closer it got to one o'clock, the more nervous she became. She had to appear calm and collected. Otherwise, Justin might sense that she was agitated, and she didn't want him to think she was wondering about the motivation of the lunch invite.

Beth arrived at twelve forty-five, and Stephanie reminded her that the library closed at five on Thursdays and to just make sure the door locked and the lights were out.

Justin walked in at one o'clock.

Was the man always this punctual? Stephanie wondered in delight.

"Hello, Stephanie. Are you ready?"

"Yes, Justin." She grabbed her purse and they walked out into the sunshine.

"Oh, it is a gorgeous day. I love all the sunny weather we have been having. It seems the days are not as hot as July was." Stephanie knew talking about the weather was silly, but she didn't want to appear anxious either.

"I thought we'd go to Henry's for lunch, if that is okay?"

"Oh yes, I like their sandwiches."

THE INHERITANCE

"Okay if I drive?" he asked as he opened his truck door for Stephanie.

"Sure." She climbed in the truck.

Justin came around and got in. Before he took off, he turned toward her.

"I just wanted to let you know that the reason I asked you to lunch today is that I would like to get to know you better. I, uh, need to tell you that the day I met you here in the library, I felt a connection, and I know that you probably are wondering so…"

"Justin, thank you for explaining, but I am happy to go to lunch with you. I feel I need to be honest with you, and while I am not sure about starting a new relationship, I am feeling a connection with you as well."

Justin smiled in return and started the truck.

Once they arrived at the café, they were shown a booth and handed menus. Trying to decide which sandwich to have, Stephanie finally decided on the ham and cheese croissant.

"Their sandwiches are all good here. My favorite so far is the pulled pork, so I think that is what I will have."

"This place wasn't here four years ago. Since I have been back, I've discovered several good places in town. I am not much of a cook like you are."

"I don't usually get a chance to go to a restaurant. I enjoy cooking and trying new recipes. John has been very easy to please as far as finding foods to make. So a lot of our meals are eaten at home," Stephanie remarked.

"Where did you get your love of cooking?" Justin asked.

"My grandma always made big meals, and when we visited, she would encourage me to cook or bake with her, so I guess I developed my love of cooking from her." Stephanie smiled.

"Tell me about your family. I'd like to know more about where you grew up."

"Well, I think I mentioned already that I grew up in Iowa. We lived in the city. Mom is a school teacher, and she plans to retire in a few years. Dad works in the business world. He puts deals together for large companies. I have two brothers. Both are still in college.

When I wanted to go to college, I decided on a teaching degree, and I also had a desire to explore, so I applied and was accepted at the University of Montana, and that is where I met Jake a few years later. He introduced me if you will to life on a ranch and country living. The first time I visited I fell in love with the open spaces and beautiful scenery."

Once their meals arrived, Stephanie and Justin continued to exchange small talk. They talked about some of their favorite things. It was comforting to find that they shared similar favorites in music, movies, and books.

"So I know you enjoy reading judging by the books you've checked out. Have you always enjoyed it?"

"Yes, I have. I used to read by the fire when I was growing up. Mom would always have a book or magazine. Dad would read the paper, and Jake would be watching some sporting event on TV. So I would find a book in the school library and read almost every night."

"I did the same!" Stephanie remarked with a wide grin. "I used to look forward to library days in school. Sometimes if Mom was able we'd go to the city library and check out books there. I used to love to sit in the overstuffed chairs at the library and read while Mom would look up projects for her students to complete and research some topic or the other."

"I remember Mrs. Stevens at the library from my younger days. She'd always greet us when we came in. Of course, getting books to check out was not always easy there. Dad didn't want to pay for a library card since we were not living in town we'd have to pay for a card—city taxes and all. So if Mom was doing shopping and Dad went to the feed store, I'd beg to be dropped off at the library, and I'd go in there and read. Mrs. Stevens would give me a bookmark and promise to keep my book behind her desk until I'd get to come back the next week. A couple of times she'd allow me to take the book without 'checking it out' because she knew in the winter we'd not make it to town as often. She always said she trusted that I'd take good care of the book, so she had no worries that I'd return it eventually. Then when I moved back here in June, I was surprised to still see her here working at the library."

THE INHERITANCE

"I know, she was a great lady and mentor to me as well. When I moved here after we got married, she greeted me the first time I went in, and she seemed to know that I loved the library. Jake understood how much I loved to read, so we had a card, and I would visit often."

"So I know then that you enjoy your job," Justin remarked.

"Oh yes, very much so. The library board has given me the full-time position and an agreement to consider some changes I wish to make to update the library. I have a presentation to give them next Monday at the library board meeting."

"Well, I am sure you will knock their socks off." Justin grinned.

Smiling at the joke, Stephanie nodded her agreement.

"I need to head home, but I really thank you for lunch today. It was very nice, and I enjoyed talking with you," Stephanie said.

"Yes, same here. I know we mentioned the connection we both feel, and I am willing to give it some time to see where it develops if you agree?"

"Sure, I'd like that."

"Next week Mike and Craig arrive and I am going to be busy with them furnishing our offices and getting ready for the grand opening, but I was wondering if you'd consider attending the movie in the park with me on Friday evening?"

"Trina mentioned that movie event to me yesterday. She said her and Brian plan to go and wondered if I'd join them. I told her that I'd think about it. I know they consider that their date night as they get a sitter for little Bobby. Maybe we could join them? Not necessarily as a couple," she quickly added.

"Okay, sure. I can meet you there. Let's say eight?"

"Yes, that would work just fine."

They stood, and Justin laid the money on the table for the bill with a generous tip added as well. They walked out to his truck. He opened the door for her before heading around to the driver's side.

On the drive back to the library and to her car, they talked a little about the changes to the town.

"I know I grew up here, but this town has made a lot of improvements, and it continues to grow. A lot of new businesses and services are available that weren't here even four years ago."

"I think the proximity to a larger city and yet the comfort of a small-town atmosphere makes it the perfect place to live. And I've only been here a year!"

On arriving at the library, Stephanie quickly reached for the door handle and thanked Justin again for lunch.

"Sure, I'll see you tomorrow evening, then at the park around eight?" Justin inquired.

"Okay, eight." She shut the door and turned to head toward her car.

Justin sat in the truck and watched Stephanie walk to her car. He once again felt that connection to her. She was a very attractive woman and friendly, sweet, and enjoyable to talk to. It shouldn't matter that she had been married to his brother. Yet he sensed that she was over aware of that fact too. He had dated others in college, but none of them gave him that feeling of excitement. He really wanted to pursue their relationship. He also wondered how his dad would feel about them seeing each other. Maybe that should be a topic for an upcoming evening. After he made sure she was safely on her way home, he turned to head toward the clinic. He needed to mark off the punch list from the contractors and make his own planned list for meeting up with Mike and Craig next week.

* * * * *

On her drive home, Stephanie once again let her mind overrun with caution, and yet she too felt excitement. Justin was a great guy. She felt so at ease talking with him. Should she consider a relationship with her brother-in-law? How would John feel about the start of this relationship? She wished she could talk things over with Trina, but once she got home, her plans for the afternoon included working in her small garden and getting caught up on household chores. She decided she would need to call Trina about tomorrow night anyway, and maybe then she could casually mention the fact that Justin would be there as well.

THE INHERITANCE

When she pulled into the driveway, she noticed John working at the entrance to the barn. She got out and waved her greeting. He returned the wave and continued on with his task.

Good, she thought her mind was too full right now, and she didn't want to alert John to anything going on with her just yet. She went into the house and began gathering clothes for a load of laundry. Dinner prep had already been started before she left this morning. Grabbing a bowl, she went out to the garden to pick some vegetables. Hopefully, the tomatoes would be ripe soon. Green beans and peas were producing nicely. She really enjoyed "producing something." Working in the garden helped to relax her.

Later at dinner, Stephanie asked John how he had been feeling lately. She really didn't want to open up a conversation about Justin.

"Ah, just fine," remarked John, dismissing her concerns. "Doc gave me some pills for the heart, and I am doing just great. No need for concern here." He chuckled.

"Well, that is good," Stephanie remarked.

They finished dinner in comfortable silence.

"I am going to go read the daily news," John told her.

"Okay, great. I am going to finish cleaning up in here. The garden is producing nicely by the way, and I want to get some more vegetables prepared for storage. So go on and enjoy your paper, Dad."

After John left the kitchen, Stephanie worked tirelessly to prepare her vegetables for canning and freezing. Saturday would need to be a full day of preparation, she decided. She decided that she would text Trina that she planned to be at the movie tomorrow evening. She also would mention that she had met up with Justin, and he expressed an interest in attending the movie night as well. It didn't take Trina long to respond via a phone call.

"Hey, so glad to hear that you will come with us tomorrow evening."

Before Trina could say anymore, Stephanie quickly responded, "Yes, I do not mean to intrude as I know that you consider the movie night a date night with Brian. I can drive myself to the show."

"Nonsense! You will ride with us. No more thought on that one. But now I am going to be nosy and ask when did you meet up with Justin and how is it he will be attending the movie same as you?"

"Trina, I have a lot to discuss with you at our planned girls' talk on Saturday, but for now, can we just plan to go to this movie and leave it at that? I promise I will fill in all your curious details later, okay?" she ended with a chuckle.

"Sure, but now you have my curiosity, and I am not afraid to say *hope* aroused," Trina added to the humor with an uplifting chuckle.

"See you tomorrow evening then, around seven forty-five?"

"Yes, we will pick you up then. Good night. Oh and, Stephanie, I just want to say I am so glad you and I are friends."

"Me too."

They ended their call.

What a long and exhausting, yet with a tinge of delight, day it had been. Stephanie shut off the kitchen lights and headed upstairs for the evening.

21

Fridays at the library were always busy, it seemed. After school, students often requested her help in locating a book or two to use as resources for a term paper or an elementary student heard about a new book in a series and wanted to see if the library had a copy. The mornings were hectic because the women's book club met in one of the adjoining rooms, and it seemed the group was always adding a new member, so the attendance was great. The chattering women were always happy to see each other and discuss the current book. Stephanie enjoyed greeting the group and encouraging their exuberant love of reading. The group asked Stephanie to see that additional copies of the book could be purchased for each member so that required being a step ahead of the group and having the newest read available when they completed their current discussion. Also, the community club held their monthly meetings in another adjoining room, and today happened to be that day for meeting as well. So the library was a busy place on this Friday when in walked a young woman dressed very fashionably and approached the desk where Stephanie was typing in information for a research project.

"Good morning," greeted Stephanie.

After looking all around the library in a practiced disinterest, the woman's gaze landed on Stephanie, and she approached the desk.

She didn't address Stephanie but waited for Stephanie to inquire of her.

"How can I assist you today?" Stephanie asked.

"I am looking for directions. It seems my GPS is not working properly, and this is the first business that I noticed, so I decided that maybe you could help me?"

"Oh, sure I can help. What are you looking for?"

"There is a new veterinary clinic opening soon nearby, and I need to find that business."

"You need to stay on the street out front and head west go through two stoplights, and at the third set of lights, you will need to turn left on Madison and take that like you are heading out of town, and the clinic is located on the right-hand side at the corner of Park and Madison streets."

The woman nodded her understanding and turned to leave the library without expressing her appreciation.

Oh well, thought Stephanie, *at least I hope she can find it. I gave her the easiest set of directions.*

Returning to work, her mind wandered for a minute on why the woman was looking for a vet clinic. Before long, school would be out for the day and students would come to the library to work on the computers and finding new books to read. So Stephanie decided that she needed to finish her tasks so she could keep an eye out on them.

At five thirty, the library was closed for the day and currently for the weekend. Stephanie got in her car and headed home. She had dinner prepared in the Crock-Pot, and she wanted to freshen up before Trina and Brian arrived to pick her up for the evening's movie in the park.

At precisely seven forty-five, Brian and Trina pulled into the driveway, and Stephanie walked out on to the porch to meet them. Settling into the back seat, she expressed her appreciation for the invite to enjoy the movie with them.

"We are delighted to have another couple join us. It will be fun!" Trina answered excitedly.

"There really isn't a couple thing between Justin and I," replied Stephanie. "He mentioned wanting to check out the movies in the park, and when I mentioned that you had invited me to join you, we decided to meet up there, and that is really all."

THE INHERITANCE

Brian continued to drive in silence toward town and only glanced briefly at Trina and reached for her hand to give it a gentle squeeze as if to say, "Let it rest."

Parking around the park was filling up quickly and finding a spot was proving to be difficult. Eventually, an opening was found. The three of them got out and grabbed the blankets, fold-up chairs, and coolers to head to a quiet area and secure a place and wait for the movie to begin. A few minutes later Brian's phone dinged with a text. He replied with a quick text.

"It is Justin asking where we are," confirmed Brian.

Justin showed up as the opening credits were appearing on the giant screen. He settled his chair next to Brian's and gave Trina and Stephanie a quick wave hello.

The movie began, and everyone settled in for a fun Friday-night movie event. The weather was perfect. During the intermission, Justin and Brian decided to walk over to the concessions for some popcorn, and Trina reminded Brian that she had packed plenty of drinks for them all.

"So Justin being here with us is nice," Trina mentioned to Stephanie and also attempting to pull more information from her as well.

"Trina, it is too awkward to talk about some things here where I feel others might overhear us. Can we please put off this conversation until tomorrow at our girls get together?" pleaded Stephanie.

"Okay, you got it," Trina replied with a smile as Justin and Brian returned with four large bags of popcorn.

Justin handed one of the bags to Stephanie, and she replied her thanks.

They settled in for the rest of the show.

When the movie ended and everyone was gathering up their trash and blankets to leave, Justin reached over and folded up Stephanie's chair for her.

"Thank you, Justin," Stephanie replied, attempting to take the chair from him.

"Oh, I've got it. I can carry them to the car," Justin added.

The four of them started toward the parking lot. Brian and Trina were walking ahead holding hands. Stephanie and Justin followed a few steps behind.

"Did you enjoy the movie?" Justin asked.

"Yes, I truly did. This is the first outdoor movie I've attended, and the wonderful night air made it an enjoyable time for me."

"Well, maybe we can catch the next one together then?" inquired Justin.

Secretly feeling delighted at the prospect, Stephanie did not want to appear too eager, so she just smiled and nodded at Justin as they continued the walk across the park.

Upon arriving at the car, Justin tossed the chair in the trunk and thanked Brian and Trina for including him tonight.

"Hey, Justin, are you planning on attending the auction at Murray tomorrow?" Brian asked.

"Yeah, I was going to go check it out. I am interested in a few items, and the auctioneers had asked for some medical opinions on the livestock that was for sale prior to the start. Would you want to ride over with me?"

"I promised Trina that I would spend some time with Bobby tomorrow as well, so are you planning on making a day of it?"

"No, actually. I only wanted to go and give my professional opinion on the livestock, maybe see a few guys and then return to town as I have to finish some things at the clinic. Plus the guys are arriving on Sunday, so I can't be gone all day, if you know what I mean."

"Okay then, yeah, I will go with you. Is that okay, Trina?" Brian asked.

"Sure, honey. But Stephanie and I have plans for lunch, so can you plan to be back by noon?"

"We can do that for sure," Justin answered.

So the guys arranged a time to meet up, and everyone said their good nights.

In the car, Brian and Trina discussed how Saturday was going to work out perfectly then.

THE INHERITANCE

Arriving back at the farmhouse, Trina smiled and said, "See you tomorrow, Steph."

Stephanie again thanked them both for the ride and the company and walked into the house.

John had gone to bed obviously as it was after eleven but had left a light on in the living room for her.

Such a sweet man, Stephanie thought as she locked up and turned off the lights before heading up to bed.

* * * * *

Saturday morning dawned bright and sunny. Stephanie wanted to make a dessert for lunch and gather up some of the vegetables overtaking her garden before Trina arrived. John had already headed out to the barn before Stephanie entered the kitchen. She hoped that John was working on the plan to hire some additional help for the farm. She would have to ask him about the progress on that later in the day.

When she was out in the garden, she heard a truck head down the road. Glancing up, she realized it was Justin heading to pick up Brian for their auction trip. He noticed her in the garden, honked, and waved as he passed on by. She returned the wave and continued on with her tasks.

Again, her heart beat a little faster at the thought of spending some time getting to know Justin.

* * * * *

At noon, Trina arrived for their girls' talk and lunch. They decided to set things up on the picnic table in the backyard. It was under the shade tree and proved to be a nice retreat for some girl time and conversation.

"It really is a beautiful day today," remarked Stephanie. "I so enjoy my Saturdays in the summer here, but if the library board accepts my proposals, I suppose I will have to give that up some."

"What proposals are you working on?" asked Trina.

103

"I'd like for the library to be open on Saturdays. I have plans to hire an assistant to work on Saturdays, but I think I will have to take my turns at working as well," Stephanie answered. "I just feel that more people might take advantage of the library and its services if they had access on Saturdays. Especially students and younger children looking for books to read or school papers to finish. I know it is summer, but there are book lists that have been assigned, I am sure. I would like to encourage a summer reading program as well."

"It certainly sounds like you have some wonderful plans. I am so happy that this job is working out for you," Trina replied.

After a few seconds of silence, Trina blurted out, "You have to tell me what is going on in your personal life as well you know! So spill it!"

Hanging her head and groaning but smiling as well, she looked up at Trina and chuckled. "I wish I knew how to answer that."

"Just start at the beginning. I will listen and comment where needed."

"So you know that Justin came into the library a few weeks ago and introduced himself as Jake's brother. Trina, I feel so guilty sometimes when I think back on that moment, but I was instantly attracted to him. Is that wrong of me?"

"No, not at all. Go on."

"He asked then about meeting up and reconciling with his father and would I help out with arranging something. So you know I was also given the festival event and wanted that to go well, but I agreed to approach John about meeting Justin. Then with John's health scare and the festival events, we pushed it back till last week. As you now know, that meeting and reconciliation went very well. John and Justin are talking again, and I have hopes for a new beginning for them to mend their broken relationship. Justin also showed up at the festival and walked me to the car one evening. He inquired about my family and how did I like living here. Oh, Trina it was so wonderful having his attention. I just feel so guilty at times. Shouldn't I still be mourning Jake? Am I forgetting all about him too quickly?"

"Stephanie, you know that I want happiness for you. I do not think for a second that you are forgetting Jake and the wonderful relationship you shared. However, I feel that you need to consider finding a new relationship, and if Justin makes you want that, then it is very good. I also believe that God assists us in our daily lives, and this is what He has planned for you."

"As you also know Justin and I went to lunch on Thursday, and it was so wonderful. We talked about how Jake and I met and he made me feel good to talk about it. He apologized for not being around during that time in his brother's life. I just can't help but worry and wonder what John especially and others too will think about pursing a relationship with Justin."

"Stephanie, listen to me. You deserve a chance at happiness just as everyone else does. If Justin happens to be that chance, then you need to take it. I am certain that John would be very happy to know that his precious daughter-in-law and his son might want to make a future together on the ranch, and it would bring him great joy."

"Oh, it is way too soon to think that there might be a future between Justin and I. I just want to feel again and right now Justin is giving me that happy feeling. I know very little about the time that Justin was away from the area. Jake told me about the arguments and expectations that were given to Justin, so I understand what caused him to leave, but now that he is back in the area and starting up a new business tells me that he intends to stay around, don't you think?"

"I would certainly think so. It would give me such joy to see you with someone and starting a new dream. We have become such great friends, and I do not want to see you leave the area either."

"How about Brian and I hosting a barbeque and asking you and Justin to come over one evening? It could be a start to hearing about future plans and give you peace of mind."

"I would like that very much. This next week is really busy for Justin, I know, with the open house planned for the clinic and his vet partners arriving tomorrow. Maybe we could plan something for the following week or weekend?"

"Sounds like a great plan then. In the meantime, you could see how John feels about you spending some time getting to know Justin."

"Good idea. Thanks for listening to me and for your continued support. You are a great friend, Trina."

The rest of Saturday was quiet and peaceful. Stephanie worked with the vegetables that she had picked from the garden that morning. John finished the chores he wanted to get accomplished and was resting in his recliner. Preparing dinner and making plans for the following week's meals always provided Stephanie with some enjoyment. She used the time to consider what Trina had told her earlier in the day. She wanted a chance to develop a relationship again. Feelings of anticipation and excitement filled her as she worked. She decided she would bring the subject up later with John at the evening meal.

"John, dinner is ready."

"Oh, thanks, Stephanie. I will be right there. I am finishing some of this overwhelming bookwork that doesn't seem to go away."

They sat down and prepared to say grace.

"Everything looks so appetizing as always, Stephanie. I am so glad you enjoy cooking and baking so much and truly appreciate you every day for it. I just wanted to mention that again," John finished.

"Thanks, Dad. As you know I really do like the cooking and baking. My grandma was the cooker/baker in our family, and I hope she taught me some of her tricks," Stephanie finished on a grin.

They continued eating in companionable silence. Then Stephanie decided she needed to be brave and speak up on what was on her mind and heart.

"So this week will be the open house at the clinic. You are still planning on attending the celebration, right?"

"Yes, I think Justin expects us to attend, and now that we are getting back on track, so to speak, I want to show a definite interest in what he is doing."

"Good, I noticed that they've chosen the first of the month as the opening day and that will be Friday. Would you want to meet me at the library around eleven, and we can go over for lunch together?"

"Sure can do."

"Dad, there is something else I'd like to discuss with you. You know how important Jake was to me, and I miss him so very much. He will always be in my heart."

THE INHERITANCE

"Oh, of course. I know that, Stephanie. I just wish you would have had more time together."

Stephanie decided to quickly continue. "I was hoping not to upset you by possibly starting a new relationship?"

"Of course not, Stephanie. I know how important young love is to a person. It makes you feel alive and happy. Have you met someone at the library?"

"Yes, I guess you could say that." Stephanie chuckled. "I am getting to know Justin a little better. I was hoping to spend some more time with him—with your blessing, of course."

John appeared to be considering that with a little surprise grin on his face. He remarked, "Stephanie, nothing would please me more than to think about a new beginning for you, and I feel now that Justin is back and starting a new business, the two of you should get to know each other. I always wanted both of my sons to find a good Christian woman with values, and I know that that is so true of you. If you think that Justin could provide you with that much deserved happiness, then I say yes. See where it goes for the two of you."

"Well, let me just say that we have not discussed a relationship in that way yet. I just feel comfortable around him, and while I don't want to bring it up just yet, I also didn't want to start something that wouldn't be okay with you."

"Well, you have my blessing, sweet Stephanie. And I will stay out of encouraging my pleasure out loud to anyone," John finished with a grin.

After dinner and cleanup, Stephanie sent a quick text to Trina, telling her that she discussed the possibility of a pursing a relationship with Justin and that John was pleased about it. Trina returned a heart emoji and a happy smile.

* * * * *

A warm Sunday service was preparing to start the next day when Justin walked in and asked to sit in the pew with John and Stephanie.

"Please have a seat," John said as he scooted over to allow Justin to sit down next to the aisle.

"Good morning to the both of you," Justin said as he leaned forward and looked across John to include Stephanie.

"Good morning to you," Stephanie replied and sat back as the first morning hymn began.

After the service ended, everyone always gathered outside for a brief visit before heading home for the afternoon.

Stephanie and Trina were standing together talking as Brian came up with a sleeping Bobby on his shoulder.

"I guess now would be a good time to head home. I will talk to you later, Stephanie." Trina waved as they walked toward their car.

Stephanie waved her goodbye and turned to walk over toward John, who was talking with some fellow ranchers, when Justin walked up toward her.

"Looks like it is going to be another warm day," Justin remarked.

"Yes, I feel that is going to be very true." Stephanie grinned.

"Your friends arrive today, don't they?"

"Yes, their flight arrives at five in Billings, so I will head over there later."

"Would you want to join John and I for lunch then today? We are having fried chicken, and there is always plenty."

"That would be wonderful. Yes, I accept that invitation."

"Great follow us on to the house then if you wish."

After getting settled in the car, Stephanie told John that Justin would be joining them for the Sunday meal.

"Great, it has been a few days since we talked, and I welcome this opportunity," John said.

At the house, John got out of the car and walked up to the porch.

"I am going to change out of these suit pants and be right back," he told Stephanie.

Justin pulled up behind their car.

They walked together up to the porch.

"Come on in. I will get some glasses of lemonade, and we can sit out on the porch. At least, there is a nice breeze out here."

"Sounds wonderful."

THE INHERITANCE

Following Stephanie back out to the porch with the lemonade, Justin again felt that strong attraction toward Stephanie and wasn't sure how to talk with her about it and not scare her away.

They sat down and Justin started to talk.

"I really appreciate the invite to lunch. I also wanted to talk with you about something. I know that we just met a few weeks ago…" he started but then stopped as John joined them on the porch.

Stephanie hid her excitement at the prospect of those words and proceeded to mention that she would begin lunch preparations and John and Justin could sit and enjoy the breeze and get caught up.

As she worked in the kitchen, she could hear the soft murmur of words exchanged between John and Justin. An occasional chuckle could be heard as well. It was such a good feeling to hear that they were starting to mend their broken relationship.

Lunch conversation was highlighted with funny stories of Justin's internship. Justin encouraged John to talk about how the farm was doing, and it all fell into easy talk as they finished the meal and enjoyed a delicious apple pie for dessert.

"Wow, I am overstuffed. Once again, Stephanie, you have exceeded your talents as a cook. I think I will go take a brief nap in my recliner if you all don't mind. Justin, we will see you at the open house later this week. I hope all goes well," John finished as he proceeded to head toward the living room and his comfortable recliner.

Justin helped Stephanie clear the table and put away the leftovers.

"I always prepare too much. But then I feel that John has access to all of this for his lunch as well."

"You are remarkable, Stephanie. You have a beautiful garden. I noticed you are showing such concern for Dad and holding down a full-time job at the library."

"Let's go on out, shall we? So as not to wake up John."

They could hear a soft snore coming from the other room.

"After Jake passed, John was insistent that I stay here, and it has just all fell into a perfect companionship. I take care of the cooking, etc. and that allows John some time to attend more to the farm. I have encouraged him to find a helping hand, and I noticed that he is seriously considering it."

"Yes, he told me earlier that he is going to hire someone soon. I am glad to know that. I know how overwhelming the farm chores can be. I have memories of that all too well, and there were three of us at the time."

They sat down on the porch chairs with their lemonade in hand. A comfortable lull in the conversation occurred before Justin continued with his comments from earlier.

"Stephanie, I just really need to tell you something, and I am not trying to scare you away or anything." He paused. "When I first met you at the library, I felt a strong attraction towards you, and it is not going away." He waited to gauge her reaction to his words.

"Justin, I have felt that same strong feeling a few times when I am around you as well."

A happy sigh and a huge smile from Justin as he said, "Do you think we could see if there is a chance to start a relationship?"

"I think I would like that as well. But please, can we just start slow? I know you are super busy with the opening of the clinic, and I am trying to make some changes at the library this week, so maybe when things settle down next week, we could do something together?"

"I love that idea!" Justin sighed happily. "I should probably head back to town. I need to finish a few household chores before heading into Billings to pick up the guys. I am anxious for you to meet them. I am sure they will enjoy meeting you. Best wishes for your library board meeting this week, and I will see you on Friday?"

"Yes, you will and thanks."

Justin left quietly with a huge grin and a wave as he pulled out of the driveway.

Stephanie sat back down and felt such a happy feeling that she sent a prayer thanking God for this chance and asking for guidance.

22

The week began with Stephanie answering several questions about a new series of books for a consistent patron. The patron was wondering if she would enjoy the series and if it was reminiscent of the types of books she usually checked out. Stephanie tried to explain how the author was a familiar one and the stories were comforting and enjoyable based on the reviews that Stephanie had read.

After finishing with the patron, she prepared some final notes for this evening's library board meeting. She felt confident in the presentation she had prepared and was hopeful that the board would see that the changes presented would benefit the library. The phone rang just as Stephanie finished typing her monthly report.

'Hello, Braintenburg Library. This is Stephanie. How can I help you today?" she asked.

"Hi, Stephanie."

"Mom? How are you? Is everything okay? You usually call on the weekends or evenings and on my personal phone."

"Oh, I know, Stephanie. I am sorry to alarm you. Everything is just great here. I was calling to see if we could arrange a visit soon? I only have a few weeks until school starts again for the fall, and your dad has decided that he wants to take a few days off and go on a road trip."

"Mom, I would be delighted to see you, and *yes*, please plan to come this way on your road trip. I think it is funny that Dad still refers to a vacation as a road trip. You would be able to stay with us at the ranch. I know John would welcome a visit as well. When would you arrive?"

"We just decided all of this last night, so we would leave here on Wednesday and arrive that evening sometime. We would stay through the weekend, if that is okay, and leave on Sunday?"

"That would be great. I have a board meeting this evening about some of the changes I want to make at the library, and this Friday, John and I were going to attend an open house for the new vet clinic that is opening here. You would have the opportunity to meet John's other son, Justin, as he is the new veterinarian now. I would also see if Beth could cover for me on Friday. She is the volunteer I mentioned once and also one of the changes I hope to make. I want her to be hired on as a part-time librarian. I am so looking forward to your visit!"

"Okay then, I don't want to interrupt your work day anymore, so I will hang up now, and we will see you Wednesday evening. Take care. Love you, Stephanie."

As Stephanie hung up the phone, she realized how much she was looking forward to seeing her parents. It had been almost five months since she had seen them. They came for Jake's funeral in January and had stayed for a few weeks as a support to Stephanie. They talked on the phone regularly, but it was not the same as an actual visit. Of course, they had tried to talk Stephanie into returning home with them at the time, but Stephanie had decided that she wanted to stay in Braintenburg for the time being. She had just made friends with Trina, and the church was so supportive to the family that she felt God's plan was for her to stay here. Now she was beginning to realize that this is where she was meant to be.

As the evening's meeting approached, Stephanie sat up the conference room for the meeting and prepared her notes. The board members seemed to have assigned seats, so she placed copies of her notes and proposals on the table.

The meeting was due to start at seven; and at six forty-five, board members were trickling into the library, greeting Stephanie as they passed on the way to the conference room at the back of the library. At seven, she closed and locked the front door and headed to the conference room herself.

THE INHERITANCE

Minutes of the last meeting were read, discussed, and approved before it was time to address Stephanie's current proposal.

"You are on now, Stephanie," remembering to call her by her first name, Ken Jackson, addressed her.

"Thank you, Ken, and other fellow board members. Tonight I would first like to bring you all up to date with the results of the town's festival results and share all the wonderful things that have occurred as a result. We have signed up several new families with library cards. New books and series have been ordered, and many new library patrons have taken advantage of the library's services in the past few weeks."

Stephanie went on to share the current library hours and many other good events that were happening at the library like Children's Story Hour. Then she proceeded to explain the proposals that she wished to make at the library.

"First, I would like to say that working as your head librarian has been wonderful for me. I have met many new people and enjoyed the programs that are currently in place. I would like to ask that we consider some changes to the library. I would like to hire Beth Johnson as a part-time librarian. She has been a faithful volunteer for a long time, and she is looking to take on some part-time work while she works on her degree. Working here at the library part-time would allow her to finish her degree and also give her some desired income. She would continue to cover my half day on Thursdays and work an additional day as needed. Also, increasing the library's hours to include evenings would allow her to work on those days as well. I feel offering Saturday openings would give people opportunities to utilize the services of the library if their jobs don't currently give them that opportunity. Improving the children's section to add more color and reading nooks would encourage reading as a lifelong habit and comfort to children. Statistics show that given more opportunities to read promotes a lifelong habit of reading, which is our number one goal for the library. We currently have one book club that meets every other week. I would like to introduce a book of the month club if you will that would be open to anyone and everyone that wants to read. Our current book club consists of several retired women, and they truly do enjoy their time together reading and discussing books. I feel older children, junior-high- or high-school-aged children, would also like to have a club to belong to. I would be in touch with the local high school to get a desired reading list of novels, and this would hopefully give the more reluctant reader a chance to participate while also completing a required assignment. Another thing is to offer monthly challenges to different age groups. Pages read for the youngest group to books read to older groups. Small prizes could be offered, and I would be in contact with local businesses to offer those prizes. I am just so excited to ask for these opportunities for the library and ask for your consideration for all of them. Thank you."

Stephanie closed down her PowerPoint presentation and returned to her seat.

"Well, Stephanie, you have completed a fantastic presentation. Might we ask that you step out for just a few minutes while we discuss these proposals?" Ken Jackson asked.

"Certainly," Stephanie replied as she prepared to leave the conference room.

Fifteen minutes later, the door opened and Susan Phillips asked that she step back in.

Ken Jackson addressed her directly. "Stephanie, we are entirely impressed with the work you have went through and the thoughts you have for improving the library. We are extremely pleased to say yes to all of your proposals with the added request that you provide another remarkable report at next month's meeting. The budget that you have requested for the improvements has also been unanimously approved, so please go ahead with those just provide me with the bills for payment as needed."

"Thank you very much, and I will give you another update at the next meeting."

The meeting ended, and Stephanie left to head home with her mind and heart overexcited. Her parents were coming for the week. She would talk with Beth tomorrow, and she knew that she would be excited. She could start shopping for added furniture and paint for the children's section tomorrow. Life was a blessing, and she was grateful for it all.

23

Stephanie was so excited as Wednesday arrived. She went to the library early to prepare for Children's Hour and to make sure that Beth would know how to cover for her on Friday. Her parents had texted that they left home this morning early and would arrive by six or so this evening. She had texted back, asking them to travel safely and again reiterating how excited she was for their visit. Yesterday, she had filled Beth in on the library board's meeting Monday evening. Beth was so excited to begin her paid position today at Children's Hour. Stephanie told her they would discuss together some planned decorative changes to the children's section when she arrived later today. Stephanie wanted to be able to spend as much time with her parents as possible while they were here, so asking Beth to cover for her a full day was also a chance to see how Beth managed the responsibility.

When Beth arrived later together, they decided on a color scheme and what furniture items would be appealing to children of all ages. Children's Hour was an exuberant time. Getting them to settle down for a story was a challenge as well. The attendance for Children's Hour had doubled and then some since Stephanie had started at the library. She often wondered if splitting the group into two age groups might be a bit more beneficial. One group could work on the art project while the other listened to the story and then switch. If asking for additional volunteers was needed, she would plan for that as well. Once school started in the fall, adjustments would need to be made for the program times.

Closing the doors at five thirty, Stephanie quickly headed to her car. She had heard from her mom about a half hour ago that they had an hour to go. She would get home and get dinner started so when they arrived everything would be ready. John was eager to meet up with her parents again also. He was in the house and cleaned up when Stephanie arrived home. He helped her by setting the table and had turned the oven to the right temperature to prepare the dinner rolls.

At a few minutes after six, her parents pulled into the driveway. Stephanie skipped down the porch steps and ran over to the car to hug her parents as they got out.

"Mom, Dad! Oh I am so delighted that you are here. I know you have to be exhausted from all that driving! Please come on in. Dinner is just about ready, and then you can relax for the rest of the night."

"Stephanie that sounds wonderful!" her parents echoed.

Dinner was delicious, and the conversations lively as Stephanie's dad told of their driving experiences and her mom talked about the scenery changes now that it was summer. After dinner, Stephanie directed her parents to their room and mentioned that she needed to go in to work at the library in the morning but would be home after one. John planned to give her parents a tour of the ranch and visit with them until Stephanie got home the next day.

Stephanie had talked to Trina the day before about the possibility of the two families getting together on Saturday for a cookout. Those plans were being arranged by Trina, who was happy to do so and delighted to meet up with Stephanie's parents once again. Friday's plans included attending the veterinary clinic's open house and meeting Justin and the other two vets. This visit would be a time for reflection and relaxation and also a time for healing as Stephanie and Jake's one year anniversary would have been on Sunday.

When Stephanie returned home Thursday afternoon, the three older adults were sitting on the front porch enjoying a tall glass of iced tea.

"Hi, everyone. Looks like you are having a relaxing time," Stephanie asked.

THE INHERITANCE

"Oh yes! We just returned from an awesome showing of the ranch, and John here has given us such interesting information about all the workings of a ranch. I for one have really enjoyed our morning," Stephanie's dad said.

"So have I," added Stephanie's mom. "It is so beautiful here and such a remarkable place to live."

They enjoyed a light lunch and then spent the afternoon talking about everything they could think of. Stephanie was happy to hear that her mom was thinking that this year might be her last year of teaching. If not this year definitely the next, her mom insisted. She would wait to see what kind of class she had this year before making her final decision, she added with a chuckle. Her dad talked about his business dealings and some of the successful endeavors he had managed. He too was looking forward to cutting back on some of his hours. Her brothers would be finishing up college this year. One graduating in December and the other the following spring. The December graduation would be a wonderful chance for Stephanie to come home for Christmas, her mom mentioned.

"Well, Christmas is still four months away, so I will definitely consider that!" Stephanie added with a smile.

The open house for the veterinary clinic was planned from eleven to two on Friday. Lunch would be served for guests, and Stephanie was excited and nervous to introduce Justin and also to meet his colleagues for the first time. After breakfast was finished, Stephanie showed her parents her garden and all the vegetables she had prepared and put away. Then it was time to head into town for the open house.

A large crowd was gathering at the facility, but it was almost as if Justin was watching for them to arrive because he managed to meet them at the car as they parked.

"Hello, so glad you are here," Justin started to say and then noticed the extra two people.

Stephanie quickly made introductions.

"Justin, these are my parents, Richard and Karen. They are visiting for a few days. Mom, Dad, this is Justin, John's son."

"Well, I am so very happy you planned your visit this week to coincide with our open house." Justin laughed.

"Well, we are too," Stephanie's dad joined in on the humor with a laugh.

"Please come on. I want to show you all the new facility and introduce you to my fellow veterinarians. We have lunch and plenty of tables set up in the back, so it is looking to be a great day."

Entering the cool building, Justin immediately took his dad over to the front desk and showed him the reception area and long hallways down to the offices with pride. Then he took the group toward the back to the surgery area and explained that this was mainly his area to work in. The tremendous amount of equipment and sparkling clean areas was very impressive.

"Justin, this is amazing. I am so impressed with all of this equipment and the fact that you will know how to use all of it. Congratulations, son!" John beamed with pride.

"Thanks, Dad. That means a lot to me," Justin answered.

"I am very impressed as well," Stephanie added as she walked around the room, checking out all of the various tools on display and asking questions about all of the machines and how they are used.

Justin answered all the questions with thorough explanations and sensible and understandable words.

Returning to the other end of the facility, Justin met up with Mike and Craig as they were exiting another group of exam rooms.

"Mike, Craig, I'd like you both to meet John, my dad. This is Stephanie." He added with a special smile and, with a soft hand on her elbow, he pulled her forward. "And Richard and Karen, Stephanie's parents, who are here for a visit all the way from Iowa."

"So nice to meet all of you. Thank you for coming in today. I am sure there will be many opportunities for us to get together in the future," Craig added.

Mike nodded his agreement.

"Well, I am so impressed with this facility, and I know it will be an honor to our community," John added.

Later, the group sat around the tables and enjoyed lunch. Justin had to leave frequently to meet other members of the community

THE INHERITANCE

and be introduced to city council members but managed to spend a lot of time as well with his dad, Stephanie, and her parents.

"Do you all have plans for later this evening?" Justin asked Stephanie quietly.

"Nothing special. I planned on cooking a meal and just relaxing, I suppose," Stephanie answered.

"Would you consider joining Craig, Mike, and me? We are heading over to Billings to go to a restaurant there that Craig discovered. Your parents and Dad are most definitely invited as well."

His face appeared so eager that Stephanie smiled in return and said, "I will ask my parents and John. But if someone doesn't want to go, it will have to be all or none. Understand?"

"Sure, I will be right back. I noticed Mike waving me over." He got up to leave.

Her parents and John were in deep conversation with a fellow rancher and his wife, and Stephanie didn't want to ask at that time. She heard Pete Marcus ask if they would be interested in bingo at the Legion that evening and noticed the happy and surprised look on their faces. They nodded in agreement but then hesitated as they turned to ask Stephanie what the plans for the evening were.

"Oh, well, Justin just invited us to go to Billings with Craig and Mike to a restaurant there, so it is whatever you wish to do."

"Dear, we will do whatever you have planned. The bingo sounds like such an interesting event as we haven't played in years. If you wish for us to go to Billings, we can do that as well."

Stephanie hesitated, but noticing the inquiring looks on their faces, she said, "I think you are most interested in bingo. So let's do that."

"Well, I have an even better suggestion," Stephanie's mom whispered privately to her daughter. "Why don't we go with John and the Marcus's to play bingo, and you go with your friends to Billings. You do not need to feel that we need to be looked after while we are here. Besides, I've noticed the friendly looks exchanged between you and Justin. I couldn't be happier for you to find someone to enjoy life with."

"Oh, Mom. I'm not sure if what I am feeling is a good thing just yet. We are wanting to see where a relationship would lead us. It is just all new for me yet."

"Of course, dear. You have rightfully mourned the loss of your husband. I think it is time for you to move on and see where the feelings take you. It is most appropriate, and Justin seems like a great guy."

Well, if you are sure, I will let Justin know. Is John interested in going along with you? I don't like to leave him out."

"I would say that Pete and Susan Marcus are really good friends and he would enjoy spending an evening with them."

Plans were finalized. Richard, Karen, and John were going to meet the Marcus' at the Legion for a promising fun-filled evening of bingo. Stephanie was going to Billings with Justin, Craig, and Mike. She noticed that the woman who had asked for directions at the library earlier in the week was talking quietly with Craig. She had arrived at the open house a few minutes before with another woman accompanying her.

Justin noticed Stephanie looking at the woman and her friend.

"That is Victoria and her cousin Abby. She followed Craig to the area. They had started an exclusive relationship back in California, and then when he made the decision to move here to Montana, she didn't want the relationship to end. I am not sure how Craig feels about it all yet. He was indicating that he might want to make it a more permanent relationship, but then things cooled for a bit right after he told her that he was moving here, so I honestly don't know where the relationship stands at the moment. I think they will most likely go with us to Billings. Are you okay with meeting all these new people?" he asked with a concerned expression.

"Sure, I think so. It is just that she stopped in at the library last week and asked for directions to the clinic but seemed rather cool and aloof, so I guess we will see how it goes."

"She can be very friendly. I suspect that she was overwhelmed from the drive and not knowing where to go or what she would see might have thrown her for a bit. I think you will enjoy meeting her. I do know that she wanted Mike to meet Abby, so maybe this is her

THE INHERITANCE

way of seeing how they will get along. I will pick you up at four, if that is okay. We need to get locked up here. I will suggest that you and I ride separately, that way we can leave if things get awkward at the restaurant. Sound good?"

"Yes," she answered with an understanding grin and chuckle of relief.

* * * * *

The drive to Billings was very entertaining as Justin relayed stories from today's visitors to the clinic. He also was so excited that his fellow vets had been given the chance to meet his dad. He had explained the whole situation to them when they had first discussed opening a clinic in Braintenburg.

"I am so sorry, I seem to be monopolizing the conversation," Justin apologized. "How are your parents enjoying the visit?"

"I have been missing them, and when Mom called on Monday and said they were wanting to come for a visit, I was so excited to see them. Our visit has been great. John took them on a ride around the ranch on Thursday while I finished at the library. Then today I was able to take them there and talk with them about our future plans at the library. Oh, and the library board approved all of my ideas at the meeting Monday evening!" Stephanie finished excitedly.

"That is terrific. I know you will make everything look amazing, and the plans you already mentioned sound very exciting as well. Congratulations," he added with an extra smile.

Again, that feeling of connection flooded through Stephanie. It felt right that she could feel happy to share special moments with Justin.

Upon arriving at the restaurant, Justin parked and asked Stephanie to wait while he came around to open the door. It had been so long since someone showed such endearing respect and consideration, Stephanie decided she was going to truly enjoy the evening.

The rest of the group was waiting just inside the doors to the restaurant. They had given the hostess their name and number in the group and were waiting to be shown to a table. Introductions were shared between the women, and Stephanie noticed that Victoria smiled brightly and said how delighted she was to meet her.

All throughout dinner, fun and entertaining stories were shared about the three men's veterinary internships. They asked Stephanie about the area and what activities that were available to enjoy. She invited them to come in for a library card if they enjoyed reading. Mike said he definitely had plans to do that as he enjoyed reading old Westerns. Craig added that he also would take her up on that but modern crime thrillers were more to his liking. It seemed that Mike and Abby were enjoying their evening together as well. Nothing was shared about how long the two women were spending here or if they had plans to return.

Overall, the evening was very enjoyable. The food was delicious and the developing friendships exciting.

After dinner, Justin asked Stephanie if she would want to walk along the path that led to a large pond in front of the restaurant.

"Sure, it is a beautiful night, and the sunset is gorgeous," Stephanie agreed.

They started walking toward a bench strategically placed next to the pond. Stopping to sit down and enjoy the scenery, Justin cleared his throat and helped Stephanie to sit.

"I know this is all too soon for you, and I agree we need to get to know each other a lot more. But, Stephanie, I just want you to know that I am enjoying spending time with you. You make me feel so content, and the feelings continue to grow for you." Justin looked nervously at her and grinned.

"Content, huh?" Stephanie added with a funny grin. "Oh, Justin, I am feeling the same toward you. I want to feel happy again, and you are giving me that in a lot of ways. I do want to pursue a relationship with you and see where it takes us. Just so you know, Trina is definitely encouraging us to go forward. My mom told me earlier that she wanted me to be happy too. I think John is accepting of us as well."

"I didn't realize that you had mentioned anything to Dad. I am so glad you have though."

THE INHERITANCE

"I just wanted to feel him out about me starting to date again, and especially if it was going to be with you, I wanted him to be aware."

"Oh, I agree. I want him to accept us as a couple too!"

Grabbing for her hand and asking if she would want to finish the path before heading back home, they stood up, and he pulled her slightly toward him and briefly kissed her on the lips.

She nodded her answer yes, and they walked around the pond holding hands.

* * * * *

Back at the ranch, Stephanie noticed there were no lights on in the house and decided her parents and John must be having a great time playing bingo. Actually, it was only nine, and so she didn't expect them back until later anyway.

Walking toward the porch, Justin grabbed Stephanie's hand and told her again how glad he was that she wanted to go this evening. At the door, he turned to face her and, smiling, pulled her into an embrace, asking if it was all right to kiss her.

She nodded eagerly.

Several minutes later and after separating slightly, Justin smiled with the pleasure of sharing several kisses.

"I should let you go, I guess. Are you okay with being here by yourself as it looks like Dad and your parents aren't home yet."

"I am fine here. But if you'd like I can make us something to drink," she asked, not wanting the perfect evening to end.

"Yes, that would be great," Justin answered, not wanting to leave either.

Settling on the porch and enjoying the night air and sounds, Stephanie told him that Trina and Brian had invited them to a barbeque tomorrow evening.

"I am sure she would love it if you would come too? It would give you a chance to talk with my parents as they are leaving to return home on Sunday."

"I would love that opportunity. I will call Brian tomorrow and invite myself." He chuckled.

Finishing their drinks, Justin once again looked to Stephanie for a good night kiss and then left with a soft wave and turned his truck around to head back into town.

Stephanie sat back down in a chair and hugged herself with a delightful sigh of pleasure thinking back on the kisses they shared. She was definitely ready to start feeling again. Everything was going to be so exciting as she looked forward to a new future.

24

Saturday morning dawned bright and beautiful. As Stephanie prepared breakfast, she was again comforted by that excited feeling of affection and caring.

"Good morning, daughter," her dad announced as he entered the kitchen.

"Good morning, Dad. How was your bingo match last night?" she inquired with a smile.

"We had a remarkable time. The Marcuses' were a lot of fun to be with. John was laughing and telling tales on their youth. We did win one game of bingo and made $50. It just was a lot of fun to go out with a group and enjoy an evening. How about your dinner with Justin and his group?" Dad asked.

"The new restaurant was amazing. The food was great. We shared a great evening together—all of us," she finished not really ready to share too many other details. She liked the feeling of treasuring her thoughts.

Karen arrived in the kitchen next. She too was happy and cheerful.

"Dad says you had a great evening, Mom. I am glad to hear that."

"Oh yes, we certainly did. Can I help you with anything over there, Stephanie?"

"No, it will be ready in just a few minutes. I see John walking across the yard heading in, so we will eat soon."

John entered the kitchen and greeted everyone with a cheerful "Good morning."

Breakfast was set out and talk around the table was all about the bingo games and the fun time. Stephanie smiled in delight that her parents and John were getting along so well.

"Tonight, we have the barbeque with our friends Trina and Brian, remember?" Stephanie asked everyone.

"Yes, dear, we are looking forward to that as well," her mom answered.

"I am going to pick some vegetables from the garden and prepare a salad to take. Would you want to help me, Mom?"

"Yes, let's do that," her mom answered.

After cleaning up the breakfast dishes, Stephanie and her mom went out to the garden. Stephanie's dad and John retreated to the barn to look over the animals.

Squatting down to pick some beans, her mom started, "You haven't mentioned much about your evening with Justin and his group. Did you enjoy yourself?"

"Yes, very much so. As I told Dad, the restaurant and food were amazing. I really enjoyed talking with Mike and Craig and the girls."

"How about Justin? Did the two of you have some enjoyment as well?"

"Oh, Mom. I just don't know if I should be having all of this feeling that I am. I really enjoy Justin's company. We share so many of the same likes and beliefs." A bit shyly, she said, "We shared our first kiss last night. Is it wrong of me to be feeling so much joy?"

"Darling, let me tell you something you may not realize. When you left home to attend college, I, of course, was lost for a bit. I was proud that you wanted to go so far away to school but knew that I would miss you terribly. I also realized something. I loved, nurtured, and cared for you for eighteen years. And now it was time to let you go on your own. I prayed that you would find a nice man who treasured you and loved you. When you told us you had met Jake, we, of course, wanted to meet him too. The weekend he came to our house, I noticed how much you liked him. In turn, he had that look of adoration for you. Then you announced your engagement and following marriage, and I had to make myself believe that it was going to be a great new beginning. You had a year of college left, and I worried

THE INHERITANCE

about you being there and him being here. You made it all work though. I was so devastated for you when Jake passed. You've picked yourself up and started over. Now you've met Justin, his brother. When you were together yesterday at the open house, I noticed a glow about you that I am sorry to have to say wasn't there when you were with Jake. I think God had a plan for you to stay here and find true happiness. Please do not think for a minute that I do not think you loved Jake. I know you did. It is just that I've noticed a true light in your eyes now. I noticed how they followed Justin whenever he got up to go meet new clients yesterday. When he asked you to join them last night, you were so eager, and I knew then that you deserve to explore this new beginning and to find your new love."

"Oh, Mom. Thank you for understanding. I just don't want anyone to think that I am pursing this relationship too soon. I am just feeling such happiness. Justin will most likely be at the barbeque this evening too. Brian and him are best friends from high school. Trina has been an amazing friend as well."

The rest of the day passed quickly, and soon, it was time to head over to Brian and Trina's for the barbeque. Delicious charcoal and food aromas filled the air as they exited from the car. Trina waved excitedly and tugged little Bobby along with her as she trotted over to the car.

"Mr. and Mrs. Briggs, so happy to see you again!" Trina added.

"Oh, please, it is Richard and Karen. And we are delighted to be invited to a barbeque. The smells are wonderful," Stephanie's mom insisted.

They followed Trina to the backyard where Brian and Justin were busy grilling on a large outdoor grill. They were laughing at something and generally having a good time together.

"Hello, folks, and welcome!" Brian reiterated when he looked up and noticed them walking into the yard.

"Hello, nice to see you and thanks for having us," Stephanie's dad said.

Justin had stayed over by the grill and was attempting to turn over items on the grill while also smiling and looking over at

Stephanie. Brian returned to the grill and teased Justin to pay attention and not to let the meat burn.

When everything was prepared, and they were ready to eat everyone took their seats around the large table. Justin managed to sit next to Stephanie. John grabbed a seat at the end of the table, and Stephanie's parents sat across the table from Stephanie and Justin. Brian sat beside Justin and Trina across from him with toddler Bobby on the end, so both parents could feed him dinner. Lively conversation was engaged and a delicious meal enjoyed as they all soaked in the warm weather and beautiful scenery.

"You have a remarkable place here, Brian and Trina," Stephanie's dad commented.

"Thanks, we try to maintain everything and take pride in the land we have been honored to be blessed with," Brian answered.

Once the meal was finished and the table cleared, everyone sat around the firepit that Brian had lit earlier and roasted marshmallows. Justin had roasted a perfectly tanned marshmallow and was attempting to give it to Stephanie, who was grinning hopelessly with the attention Justin was giving her. They appeared to be paying sole attention to each other and finally noticed that the conversation had stopped and everyone was looking at them.

"Sorry, did someone ask me something?" Justin asked.

"Well, yes we were wondering if you were pleased with the outcome of the open house yesterday?" John asked his son.

"Yes, we were. We had signed up several new clients with small animals for pet vaccines, and some local ranchers were inquiring of Mike when they could schedule inoculations for their herds. So it sounds like when we open Monday morning, we will be very busy. Which is, of course, what we wanted to happen," Justin commented.

"Great. That is wonderful to hear, son. I will need to schedule sometime soon as well."

Stephanie's parents and John were soon yawning in the night air and made excuses about being out late last evening before commenting that they might call it a night and return to the ranch house.

Toddler Bobby had already given out and was sleeping quietly in his father's arms.

THE INHERITANCE

"Yes, let's head on home as we will catch the early service in the morning," Stephanie remarked.

Gathering up the dish, they walked quietly toward the car.

"See you all at church in the morning then," Justin said.

"Good night and thanks so very much for a delightful evening," Stephanie's mom said.

The short drive home was quiet. Stephanie was reflecting on the closeness she felt to everyone there tonight. She was smiling at the remembrance of the marshmallow incident and being caught at being in their own little bubble. Good nights were echoed as everyone retreated to their rooms. Stephanie rinsed out her dish and was placing it in the dishwasher when she looked out the window and noticed Justin's truck drive slowly past their lane. Maybe he saw her in the light of the window, but it looked like he stopped briefly before heading on into town.

* * * * *

Sunday service was uplifting. Everyone there was so welcoming to Stephanie's parents and stayed to visit with them and inquire about their visit. Stephanie was sad to think that they would be making the return drive back home later today. She knew her parents were planning a stop overnight at a memorial and popular attraction they wanted to visit. She still was not ready for their visit to end. It had passed so quickly. Today was going to be a relaxing lunch and a chance to visit with her parents one more time before they left.

After lunch was finished, the three of them sat out on the front porch. John had opted to give them some privacy and was watching a game on TV.

"It has been a great visit, daughter," her dad said.

"I agree. We have seen so many things, and the people here are just so very friendly," her mom echoed.

"I sincerely hope that we can see each other again soon. I miss you both, but I also know this is the place I want to call home," Stephanie added.

No one had necessarily mentioned the date as it was the anniversary of Jake and Stephanie's wedding. It was felt, and when her mom grabbed her hand and squeezed it earlier this morning, she knew they were thinking and feeling the same thing. One year ago today was such a happy one and now a year later sadness circled the family. Stephanie knew John had also been quietly reflecting on the date as well as they had exchanged a sad smile that morning.

"I don't want to be sad today. I want to be thankful for your visit and the time we've had together. I also want to think on the possibilities for the future. I truly enjoy my job as the head librarian. I am making some positive changes there and in my personal life. I just want you both to know how much I love you and appreciate you and the support you have given me over this past year. I think whatever Justin and I are feeling toward each other is worth exploring."

"We only wish the best for you," her dad said, and her mom nodded her head with the threat of tears in her eyes.

* * * * *

Soon it was time for the luggage to be added to the car and their journey home to begin. Exchanging hugs and kisses, her parents got in the car and, with giant and long waves, left. John gave Stephanie a side hug as he knew it was hard for her to say goodbye.

A few minutes later Trina texted Stephanie asking if she needed support. She would gladly come on over and bring homemade ice cream with her.

Stephanie texted back that she was doing fine but with tear emojis. However, she wasn't going to pass up homemade ice cream!

Trina said she would arrive there soon.

Just as she finished texting with Trina her phone pinged with a voice mail from Justin.

"Hi, Stephanie I just wanted to check in with you. I know your parents are leaving today, and I am sure it is hard for you to say goodbye. Just know that I am here if you need to talk. I'd love to hear your voice. Justin."

THE INHERITANCE

She smiled and texted back that she was doing fine. Yes, it was hard, but Trina was bringing homemade ice cream, and they were going to enjoy that. She would talk with him tomorrow.

He returned the text with a happy smile and bowl of ice cream.

Trina arrived about two hours later and dished up the most delicious ice cream for Stephanie. She offered a bowl to John as well. They went out to sit on the front porch in the still evening breeze.

"Are you really doing okay, Stephanie? I know you are having a double difficult day."

"Yes, I really am doing okay. My parents surprising me with this visit this week, the great news I received at the library board meeting, your terrific friendship, and having us all over last night was amazing. I am not saying that I am forgetting this date. It is just time I feel for me to release Jake, and I am anticipating a new beginning. It is something I must do."

"Agreed. I am delighted that you and Justin are getting along so well. I look forward to many more times that we could get together as couples and do things."

"Me too."

Finishing their ice cream and just sitting in the rocking chairs on the front porch reflecting on the day and times was very comforting for Stephanie.

Later, she wished Trina a good night, thanking her for the companionship and most delicious ice cream.

She went in to spend some time with John and work out their weekly meals and events.

* * * * *

On Monday, she returned to the library and began working on the list of changes and the order she wished to get them done. She believed making a plan was the best way to get things accomplished, and it gave her some satisfaction in being able to check things off her list. She had plans to contact the staff at the local high school to get a list of novels that would be covered over the next year and offer the book club that she wanted to start as a study and tutoring session as well if needed. She researched the possibility of inviting an author to visit. She and Beth had decided on a theme for the new children's reading area, and she needed to contact a local contractor to begin the painting and building of displays. Excited for the changes, she also worked out a possible work schedule to share with Beth when she came in on Wednesday for the final Story Hour before school began the following week. Deep in thought, she was startled by the ringing of the phone and reached for it absently.

"Hello, this is Stephanie, head librarian. How may I assist you today?"

"Hi, Stephanie. Sorry to bother you at work. I just missed your voice and beautiful face and needed to see about making some plans for us to go out this week," Justin ended nervously.

Chuckling with a smile, Stephanie answered. "Justin, I am surprised to hear from you. It is opening day at the clinic. I suspected that you would be busy."

"Oh, we are, but I am in between patients, and I just needed to hear your voice."

"Well, it is nice to hear your voice as well. How about we meet for lunch tomorrow, and we can make some plans then?"

"That would be great. I will bring something to the library. Looking forward to it. I guess I better go. Thanks, Stephanie."

"Bye. See you tomorrow about twelve."

Stephanie hung up the phone and was sitting with a smile on her face when Mrs. Jacobs walked up to the desk.

"Good afternoon, Mrs. Wilkes," she addressed Stephanie.

"Hi, Mrs. Jacobs. You can call me Stephanie. How can I help you?"

"Well, for starters I am a good friend of Betty Stevens. We grew up together in this town. I would visit her here in the library, and we'd share lunch and gossip, I suppose. Then when she recently decided not to return to town and to stay with her daughter, I just quit coming in. I don't read as much as I used to although I still enjoy passing the time with a good read. I guess, I missed coming in as well as missing Betty," she finished.

"You know, Mrs. Jacobs—" she started.

THE INHERITANCE

"Oh, you can call me Dorothy," she offered.

"Okay, Dorothy, we can still offer you some excellent reading choices. I have large-print books and can order almost any book that you might like to read."

"Well, thank you, dear, but I am more into fruit trees and gardening. Our family farm is just west outside of town. We grow peaches and apples."

"How about the latest volume of *Gardener's Digest*? I just put it out on the table this morning."

"Really? I didn't realize there was a book called *Gardener's Digest*."

Stephanie walked around the desk and went to get the copy lying on the table.

"Here, take a look and see if it is something you might like to check out."

Dorothy paged through the book and eventually decided she would check out the book, leaving the library with a wide grin on her face.

Another satisfied patron, thought Stephanie, once again realizing how much she enjoyed her job and matching books to readers.

* * * * *

That evening she remembered to ask John about Dorothy Jacobs and her farm.

"Yes, that family has been in the area for quite some time. Their family farm raises delicious fruits and vegetables. When the farmers markets start up in September, they usually set up a table in the park. I knew her younger brother and sister. Walter was a year or two ahead of me in school. Her sister Catherine was in my class. When their parents passed, Dorothy and her husband took over the running of the farm. Walter left to head to the city to work in finance, and their sister Catherine went to medical school, I believe. I think she still practices family medicine in Billings. Dorothy's husband is not in the best of health, and I heard that their son was helping with the running of the farm now."

"I might like to get some peaches and apples from their stand. A fresh peach or apple pie sounds delicious."

"Yeah, it does. I know they supply the grocery with most of the fruits they sell, so it is a productive farm."

They went on to discuss the harvest, and Stephanie inquired again about John hiring on some help.

"I am looking into that currently. I am meeting with a guy on Wednesday to discuss that very thing," John added.

"I am glad to hear that, Dad. Just don't want you to overwork yourself."

"School starts next week, so I will lose my daily help. The boys are still going to plan to work some Saturdays to do odd jobs I line up for them. They both seem excited for that possibility."

"We didn't get to discuss what you thought of the clinic and Justin's colleagues since my parents were here all weekend."

"Oh, I was very impressed with the clinic. I am happy that Justin has found something that he thrives at and enjoys. I know I was hard on my boys as they were growing up. I just wanted to be able to pass down this farm to them and thus keep it in the family."

"You are way too young to think about retirement yet, Dad. I think Justin will continue to take an interest in the animals on the farm if not so much as the crop production," Stephanie added.

Chuckling at her comment about being too young, John added, "Oh, I hope so. I want him to be informed and involved as much as he wishes to be."

25

The next day at precisely noon, Justin walked into the library carrying a bag containing sandwiches and drinks.

"I am sorry, I don't have a volunteer today to cover my lunch. She called in to say her child was sick and wouldn't be in today."

"No worries, it will work out if we stay inside close to the phone and desk if needed. I just needed to see you."

Feeling elated at his words and a tad bit reserved, they sat down to enjoy the lunch.

"I don't mean to make you feel uncomfortable, Stephanie. I am just overwhelmed with these feelings I have for you. I just needed to tell you that I think you are the most beautiful and caring woman I have ever met. I want, no, I need, for you to know that I want to pursue this relationship and get to know you even better."

"Justin, you make me incredibly happy as well. I love the times we've spent together. I am looking forward to getting to know you better as well."

"Would you like to go out to dinner Friday evening? We could go to the movie in the park afterward."

"That sounds like a wonderful evening. Yes, let's plan to do that," Stephanie answered.

The rest of the lunch break they shared was spent talking about the clinic and patrons in the library. Justin knew about the Jacobs family farm as well. He thought maybe one of Dorothy's grandsons ran the horse stables north of town.

"That is something else we could enjoy. Do you ride?"

"Yes, but it has been a while. Jake made sure I knew how to ride the horses on the ranch. I do not need to tell you that I have been hesitant to get on a horse."

"Oh, I understand your feelings. The stables have trails and picnic areas we could check out sometime this fall. I am sure we could get you set up with a gentler horse."

"Sounds like a good time."

"There are bike trails and ATV trails just to the north of those stables. I've wanted to check those out too. I am amazed at all the new developments to Braintenburg since I have been away."

"Well, it is almost like a suburb, if you will, to Billings."

"What other kinds of things do you enjoy?" Justin asked.

"You know what I've always wanted to try?" Waiting for Justin's inquiring look and smile, she added, "Zip lining!"

"Really?! You are adventuresome. I've haven't zip-lined in over two years. Guess I have been a little busy with my internship responsibilities," Justin added with a grin. "Sounds like we have lots of things we can plan to explore and do together. I am looking forward to them all."

They finished lunch and made plans to get together Friday evening. Since no one was in the library at the time, he leaned down and kissed her on the lips. She was so delighted that she put her arms around him, and they shared a few more kisses before he headed out the door with a happy step.

Stephanie's mom had texted that they arrived home on Tuesday morning and that she would call her over the weekend. Glad to hear that her parents chose to spend an extra day on their vacation/road trip she sent back a happy smile.

The rest of the week passed quickly. Beth was pleased with the added hours of work that Stephanie added to her schedule. She willingly wanted to work evenings as her classes kept her busy during the day. She also said she could work on Saturdays since the library was only planning to be open on Saturday mornings. Stephanie told her they were going to try out the later evening times for a while first before adding in the Saturdays. Signups for book club opportunities were added to the bulletin board, and an ad was placed in

THE INHERITANCE

the newspaper announcing them as well. The high-school staff had returned her call and was very appreciative of the extra assistance with the curriculum. The contractor was going to start early next week to add benches, unique book displays, and painting. He said the project should take about a week. Stephanie continued to work on some new adult reading display ideas as well. She wanted to start with concentrating on a certain author and list all the available books by that author. She looked forward in anticipation of her evening with Justin too.

John had met with the potential worker and decided to hire him. He had been downsized at his company and was in desperate need of some full-time work. He had grown up on a farm and so was familiar with machinery and livestock. John was grateful for the added help. He felt God's hand in how things were coming together.

Justin and Stephanie continued to spend a lot of time together. They explored Braintenburg and all the fun it had to offer. They went to Saturday farmers markets and bought peaches, apples, and some other unique vegetables that Stephanie had not grown in her own garden. Justin spent a lot of time out at the ranch as well. He joined them for evening meals and Sunday dinners. The couple also spent time with Brian and Trina. They went to the city as well to go to the theater and attend a few sporting events. Getting to know each other and spending as much time together as they could brought them both such joy.

John had been busy pursing a companionship. He met up with Catherine Williams on a visit to the medical facility in Billings when he went for his follow-up EKG. John and Catherine had been talking on the phone a lot over the past two months. They went to a church social at Catherine's church in Billings and had also enjoyed a game of bingo at the Legion one evening. Jake and Stephanie were happy to see John with a female companion and encouraged him often to enjoy himself.

Soon it was time for Thanksgiving. They all decided that they had a tremendous number of things to be thankful for. Stephanie and Trina decided they wanted to prepare a Thanksgiving meal together for both families. Trina's parents were going to join them. Brian's parents were going to come for a bit but were also planning to go over to Brian's sister's for a celebration too. The clinic was closed as was the library for the long weekend. Mike had plans to spend the holiday with his uncle's family, and Craig was flying back to California to spend time with Victoria. They continued to see each other whenever they could. Stephanie called her mom on Thanksgiving Day and wished them a happy holiday. She was going to go home for her brother's graduation in three weeks and to spend the Christmas holidays with them. She had asked Justin to go with her. John would accompany them too, so he would not be alone for the holidays. They would only be gone for the graduation ceremony and some time to celebrate Christmas with her family before returning home the day before Christmas.

The Thanksgiving meal was delicious, and lots of conversations could be heard round the table. It was a nice holiday, but after the dishes were cleared and cleaned everyone was ready for some quiet time in their homes. John enjoyed his recliner and watched the football game on TV before nodding off. Justin and Stephanie grabbed some jackets and walked out to the pasture fence holding hands. They had grown closer over the previous three months and were continuing to enjoy their time together. Justin grew quiet and leaned over the railing.

"What has you thinking so hard?" Stephanie asked him.

"Oh, just wondering. Dad says the farm has done better this year than in previous years. The crops produced very well. Now they are preparing to change out the cattle before winter sets in. He seems to be much more relaxed since Jeremy came to work here. I am glad that they have formed a good connection."

"Yes, he is definitely more relaxed. I've noticed that he doesn't grumble as much working with the books. Jeremy has provided him with a new farming spreadsheet and program to make it all easier."

Justin turned toward Stephanie and looked her in the eye. He was very quiet just staring intently at her. She returned a smile and wondered what was on his mind.

Reaching for her hand Justin started, "Stephanie, I cannot begin to explain how happy and content you have made me, and I don't

THE INHERITANCE

want to waste another minute without telling you how much I love you." He paused. "Would you consider marrying me and making me the happiest man alive?"

Stephanie gasped, covering her mouth in pleasant surprise with her other hand. Tears started to form in her eyes as Justin opened a box with a sparkling diamond inside.

"You've made my life complete, and I thank the Lord for meeting you and starting this relationship together, and I just want us to spend the rest of our days together. I hope you will say yes."

"Justin! I…you've made me so happy as well. I love you with my whole heart, and *yes*, I will marry you!"

He grabbed her and swung her around in a circle and kissed her soundly on the lips. "Let's go tell Dad! I can't wait to hear his pleasure. I might have indicated to him that I was thinking about asking you today," he ended with a grin.

They hurried back into the warm house and approached John excitedly.

"She said *yes*, Dad!"

"I had a feeling she would. And I couldn't be happier for the both of you. God has certainly blessed this family!" John added with a smile and pulled them both toward him for a hug.

The next few days were full of excitement as Stephanie shared the news with Trina and her parents. Trina insisted that they go wedding dress shopping soon and was honored to be asked to be Stephanie's matron of honor.

Stephanie and Justin decided that they would plan a spring wedding. They also discussed building a new house on the property next to the current ranch house but not too close. They wanted to start a family as quickly as they could and begin their bountiful lives together.

An inheritance looked promising in many ways.

About the Author

Marie Malone gets her love of country living from being raised on a small farm in Illinois. She currently resides in Illinois with her husband on his family's centennial farm. Marie is a retired elementary school teacher. Her love of reading and books inspired her to start writing her own. In her free time, Marie enjoys reading, volunteering with her church, and spending time with her twin grandsons!

Printed in the USA
CPSIA information can be obtained
at www.ICGtesting.com
LVHW091204271023
762201LV00004B/864